transit

J.D. SMITH

Attention schools, libraries, and businesses: this title can be
ordered through Ingram. For special sales, email
sales@unsolicitedpress.com.

For information contact:
Unsolicited Press
Portland, Oregon
www.unsolicitedpress.com
orders@unsolicitedpress.com
619-354-8005

Cover Design: Kathryn Gerhardt
Editor: Robin Lee Ann
ISBN: 978-1-956692-43-3

For friends far and wide

contents

transit

transit

Opening his eyes tentatively, Bill woke up on a Wednesday, preparing to test a theory. With the way the sun splashed through the blinds, it had to be ten thirty. He rolled over to Cindy's side of the bed and checked the clock radio on her nightstand. Eleven-fifteen.

The smell of her breakfast, from a few hours ago, hung like a second, lower ceiling. The leftover French toast might get soggy in the microwave, but it could be drowned in maple syrup. *Real* maple syrup. When he unloaded the groceries, receipts scrolled out of the bags, listing bread priced like meat and syrup priced like Scotch.

As the French toast heated, and the ham popped and sizzled, he looked over Cindy's note. The rounded letters rolled across the page.

The second paragraph made his heart pound. "A hurricane is turning north, and it might hit by tomorrow morning." She listed the usual supplies—bottled water, batteries, candles, condoms—but listed the last one in capitals. There was more than one way to ride out a storm.

But shopping could wait until after class. Today, it was film. *Learning to Watch*, the used textbook that cost thirty dollars, claimed the best filmmakers read the world itself like a text, filtered it through their consciousness, and transcribed the results.

Looking at things seemed easy, and looking at how other people looked seemed easier. The professor had said as much.

"Then," he said, "try it yourself. Before you get up one morning, decide to be the next Quentin Tarantino and go into debt to buy equipment. Get out of bed one morning and commit yourself to looking around. See what would and wouldn't go into the frame and how it should be arranged. See if you can do it at all, let alone with a vision."

A report on that vision was due next Monday.

Today might be a good day to look; on other days, he'd lost the feeling. Bill could leave his options open by taking the 42 bus. Driving would be quicker, but the windshield turned everything into a television. Traffic dictated the pace and where to look so that nothing could unfold on its own.

*

The palm trees at the bus stop outlined stages of barrenness. The crown's green fronds wilted toward their brown predecessors. Growth turned to debris or regret, like the office buildings with vacant suites behind dark glass. Other trees sagged and approached baldness like middle-aged men. Across the city, bare trunks studded the parkways and palisades— huge, brown asparagus in a surrealist painting. But no art was involved, only a blight that curved around the Gulf Coast and palm trees that collapsed like old barns. They wouldn't weather the hurricane if it was really coming. One cloud held its place, a white decal on a blue sky.

A woman sitting on the bench tapped his shoulder. "Have you heard about the weather?"

"Yes, ma'am. They say there's going to be a hurricane."

"That's right. In the last days, there are going to be storms, wars, and earthquakes before everything is made new."

Bill braced himself against a pamphlet—or a question on whom he had accepted into his heart.

"Be ready for that time."

She didn't board with him. Instead, as the bus started moving, she clutched her sack of canned goods and walked away.

The bus windows approximated the height to width ratio—depth of field, in cinematic terms—of a screen, 1 to 1.67. Or maybe that was the ratio of the Parthenon, a fact left over from last spring's architecture class. It had been held in a building based on an eighteenth-century French plan with a miniature Parthenon set on top as if to remove any doubt as to what happened inside.

Not that any doubt existed. By night, the studio loft windows shone like insomniac eyes. By day, the building inhaled and exhaled future architects who carried rolled-up prints and poster board monuments still in embryo.

Going to a survey course with just a notebook made Bill feel underdressed compared to the majors. Some might plan postmodern townhouse renovations; others might find themselves in a megafirm, checking plans against local codes. Still some might find their work collected in coffee table books and factored into property values. But all of them had chosen their path, and all of them, on their first steps, had learned the Parthenon's ratios.

Bill would have to go check. Taking what had been offered, he sold his textbooks at the end of the term. At least a film text was on hand. He could check the screen's ratios at home, but numbers weren't his forte. Something had to be, but it wasn't numbers.

Still, his bank account shrunk slower than before. During the last call from home, in which he again hadn't asked for money, his father had praised his growing fiscal sense. Praise, like money, had to be taken where it could. A film noir character might say it was better to be lucky than smart.

Being both would help make sense of everything that came into sight. Looking at things for a long time probably helped too, and looking at them for that length of time meant loving them.

That was the danger: loving something and getting nothing back. The economists talked about the sunk costs that were followed by further outlays or write-offs. It might never be possible to know what was worth the effort, but that effort, like a word or a bullet, could never be called back.

The textbooks had left out another possibility. What if one wasn't worthy of what lay before their eyes or wasn't ready to understand it? The tangles of freeways and the adult bookstores, that dotted the blocks like oaks in a savanna, seemed like a code.

Damned if he was their Champollion—not today, anyway.

Breakfast and coffee informed Bill's muscles so that he didn't have to make an effort to sit up and clear his head. Maybe there would be space to think about what could be seen and filmed. The blocks of shotgun shacks sprawled, and the hand-painted sign at Art's Generator raised the question of what anybody needed a generator shop for.

Today's other mystery was the same as every day's mystery. For all the time they spent in bed, Cindy wouldn't show herself nude, not before, during, or after stepping fresh from the shower or over a fiberglass tub. Nude, she kept the lights off and doors closed. She reached for a sweatshirt to walk from the bed to the bathroom.

She couldn't have anything to hide. Clothed, she turned heads. In the unclothed dark, she offered drifts and dunes unbroken by scars, implant sacs, or the bones that women lay bare when they starved themselves to impress other people.

The night before, for the first time in a couple of weeks, he had tugged at a strap and said, "Please."

She had placed an index finger on his lips and said, barely above a whisper, "I can't." The same as the other times. She looked down afterward. It was no time to ask and hadn't been before.

*

The bus system's liability only included the trip and not what happened at the destination. Otherwise, today's class would be grounds for a suit. One of Bill's theories had been confirmed again—not a theory in class but a theory of classrooms. Someone had to hijack the day's agenda or the whole course. Today's someone was—against stiff competition from a rabid Francophile and a proponent of Islamic cinema—a designer socialist. Tilting back her sunglasses with the brand name of a sports car, she explained how the airplane in *Casablanca* and the sled in *Citizen Kane* were thwarted phallic symbols. She defended her analysis by interrupting anyone who disagreed.

As Bill waited for the bus home, that analysis hadn't allowed him to better understand the sight of a grackle standing in a fairy ring, twitching its black feathers. This image had to fit into a wider view, but it didn't come to mind. If it did, the problems of finding another bird and fairy ring would arise.

Maybe looking and filming had to be performed at the right speed and labeled in Italian like a musical score. The bus moved too fast to bring anything into perspective, and standing in one place gave him only a static view. A middle pace might work, and he had a world of time in which to try. Cindy wasn't coming home until late.

The bus let him off where Westheimer Road straightened into a commercial district, beginning with two massage parlors in two blocks. To the east, the female impersonator bar. Each bar, restaurant, convenience store, and antique shop could represent a world. Within them, every person was another world. A whole oeuvre could spring from the tattoo parlor that marked the land's end before strip malls shaded toward the Galleria. All the storefronts suggested now, though, was the absence of zoning.

A second sweep through the strip proved no better. The cars, buildings, and everyone in them spoke a secret language. Maybe there was no good pace for looking in Houston.

This detour led to a second one past the Greek church. He had taken Cindy to its festival a few weeks ago. The anthropologists said that food and religion were the most

8

stable parts of any culture. He had guided her through the serving line, explaining the difference between spanakopita and tyropites, critiquing the saganaki, and attempting, in vain, to convert her to retsina. The next week, he even attended the liturgy. What he had learned from his grandmother, five years gone, got him through the mechanics of lighting the candle on the way in and crossing himself at the right times, beginning with the right shoulder. What he didn't understand still sounded familiar as the incense, which smelled like the clove cigarettes that the art majors and the Europeans smoked.

Only the icons seemed strange. The Apostles and Archangels, wide-eyed and long nosed, elongated as martial artists in Cinemascope, persisted in their interrogation. The scrolls they held could as easily have read, in Byzantine calligraphy, "Why are you sleeping with this woman?" or "Would you marry her?" He didn't stay for coffee hour.

There was no point in telling Cindy this. When they drove past, she would say, "You'd better go back to your church." She didn't have one of her own.

He curled his toes and flushed the same way as he lifted weights. Someone would say that they hadn't seen him in the gym lately or—worse—say, "You're getting small." In Greek, mikro.

Every religion involved its own set of discomforts. Muslims didn't drink. Mormons didn't drink or smoke, and they had let themselves get legislated out of polygamy. Other displeasures had to go with the megachurches. Their billboards alternated with those of strip joints and featured tremendous images of tanned white men in suits next to information on how to watch and listen at home. And that was just religions starting with the letter *M*. Having no religion entailed other discomforts, like Nietzsche's years of syphilis.

A man pushing a shopping cart approached. "Excuse me, sir."

Bill sounded his watch pocket for change.

"I'm not looking for your money, sir. I pay my own way. I was just wondering if you've seen any bottles laying around."

"No bottles. I saw some cans about a block back."

"That's okay. Thanks. Somebody'll get to those by the time I can walk over. That's why I go after glass; it's my specialty. I work a little harder, and it's heavier, but glass is underexploited around here. It's my opportunity. Every bottle is a few pennies on the ground, and those pennies will add up." The man said something more as Bill looked at the church steps before speaking again in a raised voice. "Say, man. You all right? You got someplace to go? You don't want to get caught in the storm tonight."

Bill nodded and thanked him.

"You take care of yourself, now."

The man leaned onto his cart and pushed on. His scent left a few steps behind. He sang, softly at first and then from deep in his chest, the chorus of "You Can't Always Get What You Want." His specialty and his song disappeared around the corner.

*

The answering machine's light blinked once. After a long diastole, it blinked again. The bookstore or the organic grocery store could have called if they had time to check his references in Illinois.

The message instead came from Cindy.

"I just got to work, babe, but I remembered something that wasn't on the list." She recited tortillas, paper plates, and sardines—a first. She wouldn't get any competition for them.

She didn't stumble or pause the way most people did; every message was precise and brief as a fortune cookie. Usually, a recipe or a set of dry-cleaning instructions was paired with a profession of love. Her clarity came with only one condition. "Don't ever," she had said, "call me at work."

The request seemed strange—waitresses took breaks and had lulls like everyone else—but she didn't ask for much. Beyond the need for an occasional foot rub, she didn't bring work home with her, so he saw no point in intruding while she was there.

Groceries could still wait. Rush hour swirled on the expressway that led past the apartment and toward New Orleans, San Antonio, and the airports by the city's remote annexed regions, suburbs without a center. Perhaps suburbs of nothing.

Closer to him than downtown was the grocery store where he wanted to shop, a gaudy strip mall with marquee lights and a cartoon parrot whose beak begged for a cigar.

Bill made dinner or a large snack—the difference between the two had never been clear—from the perishables that would turn first if the electricity went out. Cottage cheese came first. Then strawberries. A large chocolate chip cookie followed, which was not that perishable but tasty.

Taste, like thought, couldn't be filmed, and today would not recast as cinema. The carbohydrates and enzymes carried him to bed, and he filled both sides diagonally, wondering whether falling asleep was best filmed as a fade or a dissolve.

*

Bill woke to the question of what time it was. Cindy could wake up and tell the time within five minutes. Within five seconds, she could tell the length of a song after hearing the title.

But Cindy, with her hidden flesh and perfect sense of time, wasn't available. He had no way around actually getting up and checking. It was either late or later. The convenience store sign outside the window, with its faux brand circled letter, floated its sponsored moon in the dark.

It was eight fifteen according to the clock's red numbers.

*

The car started on the fourth try, and as the gas gauge drifted up to a quarter tank, the engine growled like a dog. It was good enough for an errand but not for Galveston. If the storm made landfall, there'd be no point in going for at least another month. There never really was a point, but it happened. On nights when Cindy worked, he sometimes turned onto the interstate and passed the airport, NASA, and Texas City. He'd pass by the brothels and the other historical buildings besides the Bishop's House, but the water interested him.

The rest of the world began there. Only in the last few visits, while watching the waves bring constant news of the wind's force and the moon's pull, did he wonder what he could find anywhere else. Why hadn't he found it at school in Wisconsin or Texas, each with a different major? Those visits ended early with a drive around the sea wall and a look at the amusement park in forlorn disuse since Labor Day.

*

Bill had batteries, water, masking tape to x the windows, dried fruit, sardines, and less disgusting canned goods. The cart steadied as it filled, but the wheels still balked unlike the car, which handled itself well once it started. The third or the fourth try would be the charm.

The fifth, sixth, and seventh tries came and went. The battery was drained, and the check engine light shone an unnatural yellow-orange.

The wind cooled his sweat as he walked back into the store. Cindy would understand if he called just this once.

The number from the white pages rang twice. A man answered with the name of the bar. Nobody named Cindy worked there, and he didn't offer to elaborate.

But the place was the one she'd said. Not many businesses started with a Q, and the address in the phone book seemed right. She must have used another name to throw off stalkers or the IRS.

Waiting for a taxi, Bill watched customers come and go. They walked in straight lines and looked ahead, undistracted. He noticed a Mexican woman in a green sheath dress; the wind or the air-conditioning must have given her a chill. A woman who went shopping like this must have let her husband see her—perhaps with the lights on.

*

A silver medallion with a curved sword and something in Arabic, or maybe a passage from the Quran, hung from the rearview mirror. The driver seemed pained to take him to a bar, but he made the trip in five minutes. In a familiar part of town, Bill could have walked.

*

The strip mall's L had a parking lot of scattered pickups and muscle cars from the seventies that had approached immortality in this climate. The parkway was vegetated with compromised grass and peeling palms. A washateria and a convenience store with a different faux brand bordered the bar. Unlike the bar, they had windows.

The doorman had fat that slopped over his waistband. He sounded familiar as he took Bill's five dollars and pointed him through the curtains before he could ask why there was a cover charge on a Wednesday.

At tables near the stage, scattered men looked straight ahead. Another row of men lined the back wall. Bill took a seat in the middle, and a waitress, who was not Cindy, served him two drinks.

The beer trembled in the glasses. The first two songs had different beats with high bass, and the dancer worked to a third. She wavered from one side of the stage to the other, bending and straightening for every section of the room. She kissed the pole at center stage and stood behind it with her face hidden and a breast on either side. She repeated her previous steps with calisthenic precision. She looked only at a point on the walls near the exit sign or in a backwash of light behind the last row. As the song ended, she walked offstage and jerked a robe from a chair.

The speaker fell still and left a space for patchy applause. "Thank you, Stephanie."

"Our next performer, gentlemen, is a treat, and by the time she's done, you'll be ready to back her with solid southern support, if you know what I mean. I think you do. Let's give a big hand, and some other parts, to Miss Victoria and her Bible belt."

The bass flattened a new song. Cindy stepped onstage in a bonnet and a dress overlaid with bandoliers. Clipped onto the cartridge sleeves were Gideon New Testaments. The scuffed covers alternated between red and green. She removed her bonnet, took the small brick of scripture from her right shoulder, set it on a front table, and looked wherever Stephanie had looked. She then untied a ribbon in her hair, plucked a book from her left shoulder, and tossed it. Bill stood to catch the book but missed. He knelt to retrieve it. The bouncer near the bar unfolded his arms until Bill sat down again.

She took off a cameo pendant and another New Testament. She worked one arm out from under a short sleeve, leaving bare skin against the bandolier. She covered the width and depth of the stage in the same positions as Stephanie.

Bill opened the text, fingering uncut leaves, and in the offstage light, he squinted at the small print. He would have to wait for a ride.

interview

Stepping into a bar would have made sense; failure had no other lengthier tradition. The bartender might even have time to psychologize a little, if they did that kind of thing, before the next Blue or Orange Line train disgorged its load of commuters from DC, some of whom would be looking for a drink.

Instead, Bill walked. Sweating through his shirt didn't matter at this point. Still, bars kept suggesting themselves. One offered a five-liter beer can that came with its own tap. Another would provide a buffet of salted animal fats for people stopping in after work in an hour or so—the exact time didn't matter. A restaurant, owned by a quarterback whose knee had been shredded, also beckoned. His lower leg was reduced to a meat pendulum in a nationally televised hit. The quarterback's knee had improved; his steaks and seafood were supposedly superb.

Air-conditioning, in August, lay behind every door.

But walking seemed more important at the moment. Another block might lead to an explanation of what had gone wrong at the interview that perhaps could still be going on. The possible second hour throbbed like a phantom limb.

Walking, he ignored another block of bars because the interviewer had said, "You're a very earnest young man, but you don't have a sufficient level of training or experience." Earnest young men didn't need to take refuge in a bar during the middle of the afternoon. Not the pseudo-Irish one with an apostrophe name and a vast mutant shamrock aggressing from its sign. Nor the sports bar with several games on thirty screens at once, where he could win nothing for himself.

Where the inexperienced and untrained could take refuge was less clear.

Bill's new loafers chafed, even though they were Italian like his belt and the designer whose name graced his aftershave. The suit was not, a few hundred dollars short. Someone who had known enough to wear an Italian suit, who thus knew how things worked, might not have been considered unqualified. It had been a long time since grade school. How did that story go? "For want of a nail, the shoe was lost." The suit might have been the nail. What equaled the shoe was moot. Things, at any rate, had spiraled downward.

In that spiral, an earnest young man might pass through a parade of uniforms: from cap and gown to the present cheap suit off an undistinguished rack to the shirts and slacks of temp jobs in offices to the jeans and T-shirts of warehouses and loading docks. When that work and the clothes for it gave out, he'd wear a year-round coat and a ragged homeless beard that smelled like failure from several feet away.

Another smell, grape juice or discount perfume with an undercurrent of hair relaxer, approached before a person came into his peripheral vision.

A woman asked, "Can I walk with you?"

She matched Bill's stride before he found anything to say. The interviewer had wanted strengths, weaknesses, and recent accomplishments besides, he imagined, getting an interview after months of sending resumes.

The stranger's question had appeared in no manual.

She didn't have to hurry to match his pace. There was no place to go, only places to pass by: a small bar, a laundromat, and a currency exchange. The room at the motor inn was paid for one more night. Because he had time to think, Bill wondered whether the clerk considered him strange for checking in without a car or whether he had misread his Indian accent as sounding judgmental.

The woman shivered, rippling the floral print of her dress that was not any flower he knew. The whole garden was thin cotton. Still, walking in ninety-degree heat, she shouldn't be shivering. "Where are you going?" she asked.

These words too seemed to come out of nowhere. Who asked questions like this? The only available answer was the unrehearsed truth, at least part of it.

"Nowhere in particular. I just had a little extra time, and I thought I'd take a walk."

"On a day like this? With your jacket and tie on? You have to be hot in those black loafers."

No one else had noticed the shoes.

Certainly not the interviewer. For almost nothing, Bill had invested in a new Kiwi can and brushed to a luster two thick coats. He'd worked dabs of water into the second. With his own hands, he would fashion the foundation of his wardrobe and his career.

"I get pretty hot sometimes too," she said, looking up, smiling, and shivering again.

Bill looked down from her bare arms to her trunk, where no damp cloth cleaved to her, and past the mid-thigh hem to her bare legs. Aside from the broad scars on her shins, they were shapely but maybe a little too slender.

It wasn't necessary to speak at all. For the past week of preparations, words—like his Italian accessories, his shoe-shining labors, and cents in his pockets—had served as a medium of exchange, as the economists might say. Words for a seat assignment, a taxi ride, or an interview. More words might buy a job and more money, which would lead to dates. A sufficient number of dates—it seemed to vary—could be exchanged for a girlfriend or maybe a wife. That was how things worked.

Bill's words had been a devalued currency. They bought nothing with answers to questions on hypothetical crises, real contacts, and loyalties that must be shifted in order to work for an industry association rather than a party or think tank. In school, there had been the luxury of asking what was good. The question had since become what was good for the industry.

Not Bill, apparently, or his words.

With a net worth of forty-eight dollars and seventeen cents in cash, three-sixty on his farecard, and his depreciating shoes and belts, minus the costs of dinner tonight, cab fare to the airport tomorrow, and his student loans, he had no interest in talking. His tongue might be broken. He found no point in flaunting a fault or an outright failure, no more than rolling up his right sleeve except to give blood. No one needed to see his constellations of moles, tadpoles of hair, or Vincent van Gogh's stars, darkened.

Silence did not drive the woman away. She took in his few words the way a desert plant took up a sprinkling of rain. "You must have a nice job if you can take a walk in the middle of the day like this." Her breathing became audible. She was civil with no place to hide a knife or gun.

It would be rude not to answer.

"I don't have any kind of job." It would still be rude to leave the question hanging of why he was taking a walk, in the middle of the afternoon, in a gray pinstripe suit. "I had an interview today."

"How'd it go?"

The receptionist hadn't asked. She hadn't moved, sitting still; she may not have blinked. She must have known better than to say, sincerely or otherwise, "Have a nice day." Professionals didn't waste effort.

The man on the canteen truck at the Mall hadn't cared enough to ask either as he retrieved some local type of overgrown hot dog from its steaming bath. Though he had cared enough about what he was doing to shake the greasy water off the link and set aside the first bun, which was mashed down in the middle, to find another that was smooth and whole. Bill wondered how it felt to be whole or smooth. Because it was a slow day, the vendor didn't charge for putting on chili.

But the woman who walked beside him, closer now, was wasting effort for no reason or cared enough for some reason to waste it. Caring could only go to waste.

Bill started to explain how the interview went but stopped short. He'd had enough of sounding foolish for one day. He wasn't providing any information unless someone asked as his parents would if he called them from the hotel tonight or when they picked him up at the airport tomorrow. But this was a chance to rehearse telling the bad news and numb its sting by repetition. "It didn't go well. I didn't get the job." Heat and regret made his lunch roil in his stomach.

"What kind of job were you trying for?"

"A position as a junior policy analyst at an association." Something in him cringed and pushed his upper lip into a sneer. He no longer saw any point in using canned phrases from the want ad in the *Post*.

"That must be some kind of office job, huh?" the woman asked. "I used to have a job like that. And some other jobs."

The statement lingered for a few paces, incomplete like a note without an echo.

Eventually, it would be rude not to ask. "What kind of jobs did you have?"

"I've had a lot of them."

She slowed a little, but not from the weather, and inhaled more deeply as if to keep talking. Bill would get to listen as he had planned to listen during the interview. The personnel officer, whoever he was, had not studied the interview preparation books that said a candidate should speak no more than fifty percent of the time as Bill had. The name was already blurring, best forgotten.

The personnel officer—du jour, du toujours for him, Bill thought, in a scrap of high school French—took it upon himself to ask only a handful of open-ended questions and do most of the listening, giving him enough rope to hang himself until he was no longer a candidate for that position. Even the word *candidate* had sounded appealing, fresh and crisp with promise. Unlike Bill, who was only an earnest young man walking down an unfamiliar street with a stranger.

She had caught her breath enough to continue. "The last job I had was at my uncle's funeral parlor. It was kind of nice. I didn't have to work on the bodies or anything like that. I was typing, filing, and answering the phones."

"But you're not working there now?"

"No. I had some problems, whatever."

"What kind of problems?" There was the chance to compare and contrast the essay questions that had, apparently, led to this point.

"Some things happened. You know how it is."

"I guess I do."

"So, what are you going to do now?"

"Look for more jobs and see what happens. I'll work anywhere that pays."

"Like that place you were at today?"

"Yeah, there are a lot more like it."

Seventeen of them had sent rejection letters last week, twenty-two the week before. The pace was slowing as the possibilities thinned like Bill's hair was starting to do. He couldn't afford hair plugs, replacements, or weaves. Nor could he afford a hair-regrowth ointment or a bad toupee that a woman would eventually lift off to find his actual hair or lack thereof. He doubted any woman would want a man without hair or a job. If he looked for the punishment of approaching a woman, he'd probably hear, again, the speech that began with "You're a nice guy, but…" Its corollary would defiantly end with "Sorry. I'm already seeing someone."

Sometimes it was even true.

The speeches and their speakers ran together. He hadn't heard it or bothered to ask for it since before graduation. Her name had started with an *M* or an *N*, and she gave the nice guy speech. Otherwise, she was interchangeable with the rest, like the inaccessible jobs. All involved a desk, a workstation, and a certain facility in making presentations and writing position papers. The position was whatever would keep costs down and revenue up for the manufacturers as opposed to the unions, the unions as opposed to the manufacturers, or both together against the environmentalists, who were on their own.

Survival wasn't good business. The green groups had provided his first round of rejections, even before the human rights groups. They were followed by rejections from the non-partisan think tanks favored by either Republicans or Democrats. And now from the associations, whose funds drove both. Even that would have been better than going back to the grocery store and putting on an orange vest that had made him look like a chimpanzee.

If the job wasn't perfect—and no job was—some consolation had to lie in eating lobster whenever you wanted, drinking wine that came with a cork, and maybe having an apartment with no roommates just for the hell of it. If the job to pay for it could be found. Which, at the moment, could not be found.

A drink from the liquor store across the street or a half-empty bottle in front of the storefront church was becoming what employed policy analysts might call a viable option.

"Did you have your heart set on this job?" the woman asked. She smoothed out her hair with several short, quick strokes.

"Not really. At this point, I'll work for anybody."

"Me too."

"Who would you work for?" Bill asked.

"You."

She must've had a lapse in memory, or maybe she hadn't been listening that well after all. "I wish I had some work to give you, but I don't. I'm sorry."

Bill heard his unweighted words and believed them. Abundance would lubricate his every dealing, if it ever came his way, but that didn't seem to be in the offing.

"Sure you do," the woman said.

"What do you mean?"

She pointed to the intersection of an idle loading dock, a cluster of bushes, and a dumpster on the next block. "Let's go over there, and I'll show you what I mean."

She would have to. This didn't seem like any familiar business. But it wasn't as if he had other commitments. They were already heading in that general direction.

"How about it? I'll give you a blow job. It'll only be fifteen dollars."

Bill stopped, and she passed him by half a stride before she stopped and turned around.

"Wait a minute," he said. "I don't know about this." A flat no would be rude and final. He knew. He had been on the receiving end.

"You can get to know about this if you want." She pulled down her dress' cotton strap and drew it down and out. There was no second strap beneath. "Come on. I won't bite down on you or anything."

"This doesn't sound right."

"You won't catch anything. I'm clean. I'll even give you something to put on." She seemed to have trouble focusing on him. Each eye looked straight past him to no place in particular.

"I can't do this." To walk ahead or away would still be rude.

"Sure you can." She reached for him without raising her arm.

Bill stepped aside but did not lift his pivot foot.

"You're tougher than you look. Ten dollars."

Forty-eight dollars seventeen cents minus ten dollars, a debit to petty cash, and a credit to recreation or physical development, which is something he'd taken once in an attempt to be practical according to the precepts of his accounting class.

"It'll only take a minute."

This did not strengthen her position.

"Please." She keened as if she'd been struck. With a blink, her eyelashes were wet. Being arrested for an assault that hadn't taken place seemed possible at this rate.

Bill scanned the next block of vacant lots and the storefront whose sign welcomed food stamps to see if anyone was looking. "What you do when no one is looking," his father had said before, "shows your character."

"Please." This time, the word seeped through a sob.

Everybody needed money; there was no getting around that, but it seemed strange that she needed fifteen dollars badly enough to settle for a sure ten and hope for the remaining five to come later. She didn't say anything about having a baby or a dog as the homeless did. She was thinner than she needed to be but not emaciated.

Ten dollars would buy her a hamburger or two, though. If that's what she would buy.

Bill couldn't imagine that kind of need, at least not yet. It was worth the ten dollars to have it out of sight. The five dollars he saved could buy him a drink at happy hour. He could use one. "I'll tell you what. You don't have to do that. Let's say I just give you ten dollars, and you go on your way."

Her need broke into his accounting. "I'm not a beggar. I want to earn my money." She tried not to shake but failed, trembling as if she were being shaken hard by an invisible hand.

"Really. You don't have to do this." He couldn't think of why not. People wanted to work. Sex with her, or with anybody, would be the icing on a cake that did not exist.

He didn't have to give her the money. He could walk away or outrun her if she yelled. He wouldn't look like the bad guy. He wouldn't even *be* the bad guy. Still, rejection had

27

already stained him once today on the receiving end. He didn't want to stain himself again by spreading it out.

From his father's counsels, numerous and useful, came an explanation of why he had dropped out of a fraternity when the hazing began and why Bill should not join one to begin with. "Life"—that was just how sayings began—"is not a conveyor belt of shit. Just because you get dumped on doesn't mean you get to dump on the next guy who follows you. You don't see me yelling at your mother when I've had a bad day at work."

He was right. Bill hadn't seen that, and he didn't pledge or even rush.

"Please." The next wave of tears pulsed like blood from an artery. "I'm not worthless. I want to work." She wasn't a candidate for anything either. She was a colleague. "I'll be good. I'll be real good." She looked down at nothing in particular. "I'll treat you nice."

She faltered as if she'd come to a gap in a marketing script just like he had a few times in order to pay for the airfare and the hotel.

But she recovered. "What's your name?"

There was nothing to gain by any other name he used; he had nothing at stake now. He told the truth.

She took his hand. Looking down still—the path must have been familiar—she led him toward the intersection of the loading dock, the dumpster, and the cluster of bushes.

The walk gave him time to think. He would have to ask the woman's name; it would be rude not to.

He owed her that much at least.

the suburbs of greece

Bill Basil, who did not smoke, coughed out a lung-sized cloud and resolved not to inhale the next puff.

"It's okay, boss?" asked the taxi driver, who drew on his cigarette as if the smoke were a sea breeze.

"It's okay," Bill said before he could think. Maybe it was. Compared to breathing in Athens, which had to equal two packs a day, an unfiltered cigarette or two posed little threat compared to the risk of insulting the driver, who could drop him off anywhere, demand all his cash, and take his American passport. A little smoking was an acceptable risk. No bus ran this way from Tripoli, and there was no car rental. A taxi was the only way to the ancestral village. Being called "boss" had its points too.

Bill had barely finished approving his own judgment when the taxi swerved left to avoid the flock that bulged ahead of their shepherd and made a hard right to escape an oncoming truck.

The driver let out what sounded like curses on the livestock, the truck, and perhaps the highway's mere two lanes, exhaling a blue-gray cloud. As he straightened the car, he looked over to Bill and reassured him in their shared vocabulary. "It's okay."

Bill couldn't disagree, even when the driver swerved again as he took one hand off the steering wheel to cross himself as he drove past a church at, give or take, one hundred and ten kilometers an hour—sixty-eight miles an hour or so if

Bill was doing the math right. No problem on Interstate 80, but on curves and cracked pavement the speed raised a few questions.

The landscape came fast enough to resemble the murals on Halsted Street with their restaurant walls of blue sky, white stone, silver-gray olive trees, and flocks of off-white sheep like low clouds. They were ubiquitous as billboards on the highways around Chicago. The landscape left fast enough to escape serious comparison.

But it was okay because this was where it all started. There was the maternal line who had always seemed to be in America, like the Capitol or the Liberty Bell, who had always spoken English, but they faded into him from the far end of a continuum that began somewhere behind the horizon.

The Basil line, originally Vassilopoulos, had a before and after. His grandfather who crossed the Atlantic had his name cut by three syllables and achieved some success. Vassilopoulos. Bill tongued the five syllables against the roof of his mouth and guessed the cost of a name change when he flew back. His leftover traveler's checks would cover the price of the court proceedings and legal notices.

The driver had held a straight course for a few kilometers. But now, he slowed just enough to cut a hard right turn without fishtailing and slowed further as the road diminished to gravel. Past a few clusters of stucco houses in the dust outside a church, the taxi coasted to a halt.

"Eimaste edo," the driver said. But when Bill did not respond, he added, "We're here, boss."

"Nai," Bill said, meaning *yes*. He reached for his wallet in his back pocket but found it in the front pocket, where a pickpocket would have to work for it. "Posa?"

"Two thousand five hundred," the driver said with a clear command of English numbers.

Bill had no way of knowing if that was a good or bad price. He could afford it though, and he paid, adding another five hundred drachmas for a tip and an American single out of impulse. When the cash left his hand, he remembered a final detail: getting back to Tripoli. He pointed to his watch and to the late morning sun and tried to make a reservation for the taxi's return at one thirty or thirteen thirty. One of the two had to make sense. In case they didn't, he wrote the time on a sheet from his notepad and said, "Here." Then the word came back to him. "Edo."

The driver refused the sheet. "Okay. Ena trianta. Edo." He made a wide loop around the plaza, grinding out his own low cloud of gravel and dust, and left the village in seconds. There wasn't that much village to leave anyway.

Bill adjusted his daypack and took in where he stood. He was most definitely edo—Kalokerassia. It garnered the smallest dot on the Michelin map, and it appeared on no other. "One-horse town," his grandfather had said in the manner of the Westerns he watched. "Nice place. No work."

Bill saw both truths as he struck a course through one main street of two. On the opposite side, the New Democracy Party's office stared down the Communist Party's office. On the New Democracy's side was a pharmacy; they also had a pharmacy on the Communist's side: a tobacconist. All four seemed to manage without staff.

The street did not end so much as it curved and narrowed into a hillside trail. Because it was new, Bill followed it up a ridge that rose toward the terraces of olive groves. The trail deteriorated as it rose and turned into loose gravel and live rock, too smooth to find a foothold. The trail also grew steeper. He pulled himself up by an anonymous, arid root when from the corner of his eye he saw an old man descending.

Bill pivoted off the trail and into grass and brush, still holding onto the root, as the old man and his donkey approached.

"Chairete," Bill said, wondering what the greeting meant in more precise terms.

"Chairete," the old man said without slowing as he led the animal down what must have been the trail's sweet spot.

Bill still wondered about the word's translation as he grappled around a bend and looked up just in time to clear the trail for another old man and his respective burro.

"Kalimera," Bill said. Good day. He again heard himself echo, without a Midwestern accent, in the old man's voice. This old man also led his burro downhill without breaking stride or a sweat. His arms and legs were as thin as the soil and as lean as the olive branches.

Bill clambered farther up, sweated, and caught his breath. His limbs felt thick and heavy like the humus of downstate Illinois even though he was not old.

The trail kept rising, and Bill's legs grew tight. Pausing to catch his breath, he realized the clock would save him from following the trail farther up. He wanted to walk where his grandfather, but he had to be down in the square by one thirty, or he'd end up stranded.

Bill turned around and took in the village. First, there was Greece. Then Chicago, where there were more Greeks than anywhere outside of Greece. Then the suburbs of Chicago. Each move came from necessity or opportunity. If the outlying areas here were the suburbs of Chicago, then perhaps Chicago was a suburb of Greece.

With that thought, he made his descent, surfing down a few patches of loose gravel when he lost his footing and returned to the square. The two old men and their respective burros were nowhere to be found. He had yet to see a horse.

The taverna—he knew it from pictures of others like it and restaurants modeled after the pictures—was the only place left to go. Bill found a seat at an outside table. As he set his daypack at his feet, something that sounded like thunder cracked the blue sky. He winced, looked up at its source: a fighter jet. It was the kind whose name began with an *F* and ended with a number. It would bank hard and fly out of sight in seconds. He knew an air base was in Arcadia.

Recovering his composure, Bill found a middle-aged waiter standing beside the table.

"Kalimera," Bill said.

The waiter answered in kind but said nothing more.

He studied the paper menu like a cue card, transliterating the letters and words. A semester of the language could only sink in so far. It was not taught at home. "Here we speak English," his grandfather had said, while never mastering it.

"Salata, psomi, kai krasi," he ordered.

33

The waiter left before he could finish the last syllable.

Waiting, Bill wished that he smoked, so he could have a conventional way to pass the time. He looked around instead. At the ridge, he saw where he had scaled part of the way—a small part—with the jagged mountain behind it. He looked at the houses, neat and trim as matchboxes, but the stucco and the patios behind them, shaded with horizontal trellises, were bound with vines that dangled in clusters of green grapes. His grandfather had mentioned this much. They hung in uneven branches like the testicles of an alien life form. His grandfather had not made that comparison, though.

Bill also looked at the other customers. He noticed two old men as weathered and sturdy as the ones he had seen on the trail. They carried on a vivid conversation over their ouzo, and in the midst of it, only one word besides articles and names stood out to Bill. In the center of a long pause, the shorter of the two said touristas as he looked Bill's way, spitting out each syllable like an olive pit.

Lunch came with the check next to it. The ticket equaled two dollars and thirty cents, give or take. In Chicago, that kind of money couldn't buy a single glass of wine.

Bill ate and drank, and in the wine's creeping glow, he resigned himself to not seeing Kalokerassia's single horse. He was braced, though, for the jet's next sortie. What lay before him was enough. He could master the language if it bought him relief from a Midwestern winter. Perhaps he could, through a good word from a fourth cousin or a fourth cousin's friend, find a wife. He'd heard that these things happened.

As if he had read Bill's thoughts and was prepared to take another order, the waiter returned to the table. Bill rounded up and paid about three dollars American. With all three customers served, the waiter stayed to talk.

"Are you Belgian?" the waiter asked in French.

"Non," Bill said. Another semester, another language, had come in handy.

"Are you Swiss?"

"Non," Bill said, "Je suis américain." He added, in Greek, "But I have family here."

"In Greece?" the waiter asked in English.

"Here," Bill said, encompassing the village with a sweep of his hand. "In Kalokerassia."

On some unseen dime, the waiter's thoughts seemed to turn. "What is the family name?"

"Vassilopoulos."

"Several people have that name here." The waiter called over to the old men. "Yiorgo, Bartolomeo. Elate edo." The old men approached, and the waiter said, reverting to Greek, "This young man is your cousin."

Bill found his hand seized in turn by the two men's rock-hard grips and the rest of his person embraced before he could stand up to show them respect. He scarcely had time to gather up his daypack before they almost herded him across the plaza toward one of the trim, squarish houses.

"This is a big thing," the waiter said behind him. "For years, this doesn't happen."

The men passed him through the door and seated him at the head of a kitchen table. There was a flurry of speech, too fast for Bill to grasp more than scattered words broken out of

35

context. Female voices joined in. Soon, two older women, who must have been grandmothers, emerged from some corner that the house seemed too small to have. One set a huge slice of watermelon in front of him. It crowded the table with its smile of red flesh and black seeds.

The woman who served him spoke. "You are Vassilopoulos?" she asked through the waiter's interpretation.

"Yes," Bill said. To explain that the name had been Americanized seemed like a digression, perhaps even an insult.

"Are you the grandson of Stavros?" asked the other woman, again through the waiter.

Bill shook his head. To say Oxi, as Greece had said to Mussolini in 1940, seemed rude.

More questions came from everyone. The waiter lifted his hands first out of frustration and then to direct the verbal traffic.

"Are you the grandson of Odiseos, who went to Alexandria first?"

"Are you the grandson of Chrysostomos?"

"Are you the grandson of Charalambos, who got rich from his restaurants?"

Bill had heard of the first two but not the third.

"Are you the grandson of Aristoteles, who went to the university?"

Several more possibilities passed by him. None matched.

"You have to tell us then. Who was your grandfather?"

"Dimitrios."

"Dimitrios?" The waiter seemed perplexed.

"Yes, Dimitrios."

On another unseen dime, the waiter turned and the rest of the room with him.

"Dimitrios," the waiter said, "seduced the priest's wife."

"Dimitrios," said the woman who served him, "raped the sheep."

"And the chickens," the other woman said.

"He stole wine from everyone's barrels."

"He soured the milk by looking at it."

"Because of him, the crops failed."

"Because of him, the Germans came."

Bill understood more than he expected.

"Dimitrios was a curse."

"And our curse is on him."

"And on his descendants."

"You," said the man who'd labeled him touristas, "get out of here now."

The other old man stepped out of the room. Somewhere rested the knife used to cut the watermelon.

"Bastard," the waiter said as Bill gripped his daypack and stood up.

"Malakas," said others as he backed to the door.

Before turning to run, he saw the second old man return to the room.

He reached the middle of the plaza in seconds. He had nowhere else to go and hoped no guns were in that house.

The shouts reached him. The men filed out of the house as the taxi came. *To the rescue*, Bill thought. *Sweet chariot*, as the song went, *coming for to carry me home*. In a movie, no one would believe this, but stranger things had happened just moments before.

He yanked open the door and told the driver, in Greek, "Go fast!" He did not know how to say, "Step on it."

The driver whipped the car around as he offered Bill a cigarette, which seemed even less dangerous this time. Bill lit it up as he monitored the village in the rearview mirror. In that instant, America looked good. Chicago looked especially good, even if every street and sidewalk was covered with slush.

produce

Only onions posed a problem. The mushy plums could go. Buying them was a habit carried over from when Maris was still in town. Bill would buy a pound or two, forgetting she had left or wanting to remind himself of her as if that would help anything. Hell if he knew one way or the other. Keeping them around wouldn't bring her back from Atlanta or wherever she lived now.

The tomatoes could go as well. The hothouse beefsteaks turned into mush, and the grocery-store hybrids had never gotten ripe.

A dispersed salad lined up. A moldy peach and a handful of black walnuts from the park would add variety. No eggs.

Bill set the TV tray of produce on the balcony as a bat shrieked by. The mosquitoes it fed on had been in the air since twilight. Bats had their job, and he had his.

Tonight, that job involved choosing onions. Vidalia onions were golden with the sulfur of their Georgia soil, the just right porridge of onions. The best had the size and heft of baseballs, and he could lob like them like a warning shot near a car cruising for crack or hookers. Once or twice, he had come close to hitting dealers pushing their lieutenants around and slipped inside before the word *motherfucker* and its variants spangled the air. Stupid bastards.

The pleasure of condescension ended as blood and shame rushed into his temples. He was missing the point as much as they were. The point was to love, not judge. If he wasn't going to teach them something, he could just as well stay inside. Anything else was vanity. That particular onion couldn't revive a shriveled body in Sudan or whatever starvation's stop was on its never-ending world tour, but throwing it for no good reason was a waste, an insult to nature. If he wanted an onion later and didn't have one, he had no one else to blame.

Bill set out the tumbler. Heavy-bottomed, it must have started life in one of the proverbial better department stores or an upscale bar, passing through homes and being chipped en route to the thrift shop where he'd found it behind a thicket of mismatched wine glasses.

He pulled the bourbon out of his cupboard from between the black beans and the ramen packs. Cutting corners on food and housing had stretched out his money during his leave of absence while he sorted things out. Still, all his cutting corners and sorting things out might end with nothing to show for the trouble. Next week was the deadline for going back to work or resigning. Fish or cut bait. Everybody—especially a copywriter—could be replaced.

It would come down to whether he had enough money to hold out for another job and more time to think. Figuring out the finances could wait until tomorrow. Running the numbers drunk sounded like a bad idea.

Tonight wasn't making them any worse. Drinking at home was cheap, and there was only one bottle of whiskey here. He had wine to go with dinner. Jug red worked with all kinds of canned soup, as well as omelets. He would also grab beer on the way home after running errands. But he kept a house rule: only one bottle of hard liquor at any given time. No back-ups.

The time for beer and wine, though, had passed. It was nine o'clock.

The first shot went down fast. Then the second. Aligning his throat and the glass sent the whiskey straight down like tipping a can of oil spiked with the spout, or whatever it was called, into the crankcase. There had never been time to wonder about the word *before*.

Now he had time to study words and everything else. Outside, a few rounds popped with a pause between them, but they hit nothing. Only a semiautomatic. He didn't have to become the beast he fought, but it was hard not to turn into a kind of zoologist.

Before things with Maris fell apart. If they'd been married, they would have been goods or money to divide. So many dollars a month would have served as a symbol of separation and penance. There was only blame, which didn't split into percentages.

Some must have belonged to Maris. She could have been something other than oblique—or was it opaque—with his attempts to start the Talk with a capital *T* or what his friends called the "what are we?" talk. His friends had already decided. If it looked like a duck and walked like a duck, then he probably had a duck on his hands.

Ducks were harder to identify up close. Once she suggested returning to a vegetarian restaurant that they had tried a few nights before. It wasn't going to happen. Anonymous beans and grains, paste, and sawdust under a veneer of curry still lay on his tongue. "Not that crap again."

She laughed and looked across the kitchen table. "Are we having our first fight?" *Quack?*

They had ordered a pizza and sat inches apart on the couch. For an hour, he stayed on his side of the invisible plane between their cushions, and after that hour, he left.

There was no telling if anything could have been salvaged. Within a week, a neighbor, already half drunk, had invited him up for drinks, and they fell into bed without dinner. There was no time to call Maris and see if she would have cared. Besides, she had something coming after all his frustration. For a month, he had no time to call, but he did erase her messages from the answering machine. When the neighbor stopped answering her door and telephone, the affair dissolved into itching, recrimination, and an edge of Kwell in the shower's steam.

Then came Maris' turn to not answer his calls or notes left on her windshield. When he tried stopping by—only on even-numbered days to show he had some restraint—she apologized for having no time to talk. When he finally did have time, he took the opportunity to propose on the spot. She answered at once. "I think you should leave now." If the police came, they weren't going to help him.

Several months later, they ran into each other at a department store, and Maris was not the first to ask if he had AIDS. As Bill told everyone truthfully, he had only lost weight. she retreated to the lingerie section.

That evening, a recorded message declared her number changed and was unlisted. Another car parked in front of her house, and the front room's amber light outlined new furniture. Another weekend without eating followed, and

42

Monday began with vomiting. He had dry heaves at first but then an emerald of bile.

Time for a refill. Then another, a choice of missile. Close by was a wizened tangerine, shrunken in its peel like an old man in his clothes. Its three or so ounces could cause problems with terminal velocity and being knocked off course by the wind. Navel oranges, with cork-thick skin and moist segments, didn't present this problem, but they were worth eating, which he'd done for the last month. It would have been ten weeks, the longest streak except for a two-day lapse near Maris' birthday. Or was it the neighbor's, whose name had dissolved after the second drink?

Bill was ready to go for a knuckleball, so definitely the tangerine. His hand wasn't big enough to wrap that way around an orange. He had made the right choice, for once, of what to keep and what to throw out. Did that come from an ethics course or an econ course? Either way, it was the opposite of how he'd handled things with Maris, and the distinction didn't help at the moment.

Live and learn. Then live, whether or not there was any chance to apply what he'd learned. Or he could stop living. That was also an option. For pussies. How could he know if he'd learned anything without waiting to try it out? He couldn't leave a mountaintop or the moon without at least trying to plant a flag.

That would be like ignoring the woman who might have loved you, inscrutable as she was, and sleeping with someone else.

A professor had once laid out the difference between the two schools of ethics. One went for the end justifying the means if it came to that, but the results kept slipping into the future. When would you know the final results? The other approach meant doing something because it was the right thing to do, whatever the results were.

Bill aimed the tangerine in front of a cruising SUV that swerved and then slowed. A tinted window rolled down at a stately pace. One voice shouted something garbled, and another said, "Hey, watch where the fuck you're throwing shit."

A low-caliber round nicked a cinder block on the next floor. Was this their warning or just bad aim? A quick read of the day's crime news suggested that most of the punks out there couldn't shoot worth a damn and just kept pulling the trigger until they got lucky.

Still, throwing the tangerine may not have been a great idea. The SUV sped up and turned the corner before a sure answer suggested itself. The questions and answers were always a step behind events or, in the case of Maris, months behind. How could anyone know what was the right thing to do?

The law dealt with intent. But that went back to consequences. How could anyone tell if the intentions were any good?

There had been time to read about the issue since both Maris and the neighbor were gone with no successor in sight. Rehearsing introductions and pickup lines at home didn't help. The words, sometimes read from index cards, stopped in his throat.

Worse, he said what he was thinking. "I just made the biggest mistake of my life." Then came the fucking tears again. There was no way to go out or to go to sleep. Instead, he read to see if there was anything to learn from his mistake.

The Desert Fathers had covered ethics in biblical language: discernment of spirits, testing all things, holding fast to what is good, and so on. The right thing could be done for the wrong reason, like rescuing a drowning child to be known as a hero, and a man who resisted temptation could still be wretched. Was a man who stayed out of brothels primarily to protect his reputation any better than the man of no reputation who went in?

Bill only threw fruits and vegetables near the johns, whose demand drove the trade, and not the hookers. He didn't want the johns to debase the women—or themselves for that matter—by treating people only as a means of pleasure. The women had it bad enough already. Presumably none of them had listed this as what she wanted to be when she grew up.

After shot five or six, he lobbed a few bruised apples in front of the dealers' front men, all under eighteen for catch and release in court. Some of the shorties were already six feet tall, but they still had time to look for a new line of work before they could be tried as adults for slinging their goods or taking a shot at someone. Like him.

Which he had avoided so far. To seek out martyrdom would have been to act from pride or a love of praise, even if he didn't live to hear it. More likely, if nobody could figure out why he pitched groceries off a balcony, it merely made for a stupid death like the man in Manila who had been shot in an argument over whether the chicken or the egg came first. The stories never said what side he took.

The SUV turned left onto the street and stopped in front of a fire hydrant. Two men stepped out. The guns were no surprise, but the banana clips were. They were good for at least fifteen rounds.

Bill jogged into the kitchen and jogged back out to wait.

He had no time to call the police. He tossed an onion in front of the men. He crouched behind the railing and came up with the mesh bag. He threw again so that the men would stop and think. He threw again after that.

Onions arced and dropped to the sidewalk, choice after choice.

fables

no redemption without blood

Panayiota was the village slut. Everyone knew. Once, she was even pulled out from under the priest's son, Costas, who was known to prefer goats and boys. Her dress was wrinkled and prickly with straw. It was only a matter of time before she took up her trade and became the village whore. For the men, this was a great stroke of luck because Katerina, who had done the job for fifteen years, was getting crow's feet and rolls of fat.

Most of the boys already said that they had been with Panayiota. Others smiled and said, "Not yet." There was no point in asking Panayiota herself. Someone with so many sins on her head would just add one more and lie about the rest.

No man would marry such a woman since she would be used goods or since others were still using her goods. Even a dowry could not help.

A shabby future waited for her, and day by day, she approached it with swelling breasts and hips after working long hours in the vineyards and the fields. On market day, she had to lay down her coins before anyone would pick them up, lest the vendors touch her hand. When she walked away, women would spit where she had stepped. Men would spit, follow her with their eyes, and spit again.

When Panayiota was twenty, and other girls had long since married and had their second or third child, a stranger named Yiorgos came to the village. He said his father lived far away and had sent him out to work. Sometimes, he healed the sick, though no one knew where he had learned his skills. He sold fish even though the sea was a day's journey away.

Unlike others, Yiorgos took money from Panayiota's hand, and when she left, he did not spit.

They took walks in the square. No one dared to follow them closely enough to listen; everyone had an idea of what they talked about: when, where, and how. Some guessed at a price.

Catching Yiorgos with Panayiota would prove what was already known about her and explain why a stranger would come to this village. They would be pierced with a single sword. Yet whoever looked for them at night would only find Yiorgos alone in his rented stone hut, grinding herbs, praying, or eating a piece of bread for his supper.

Yiorgos disappointed the village again by marrying Panayiota after the priest saw that he had no hooves or horns. The only witnesses for the ceremony that could be found were Katerina and a man who could have been one of Katerina's first customers. He talked to himself about his visions all day or talked to the visions themselves. His nose had long since fallen away.

Once Panayiota moved her things into Yiorgos' hut, the people set up a vigil outside. By dawn, any decent couple would drape the window with bloody sheets to prove the bride's seal had been broken for the first time. No one could guess what a couple like Yiorgos and Panayiota would do.

Hours passed, and the hut stayed dark. No one could hear a sound from inside, and no one dared to come close. The people waited, talked, and grew bored. Some grew so sleepy that they convinced the owner of a kafenio to open in the middle of the night. For his trouble, he charged a little extra on each cup. He made a great deal of money that night.

The moon and stars crossed the great sky, and some wondered if the newlyweds had slipped away.

The morning's first birds may or may not have been singing when the curtains parted. A sheet was hung like a banner, scarlet in the right places.

The people gasped and murmured. A slut and a stranger could not be allowed to make a fool out of everyone else or to make a mockery of tradition. With a few strong men in front, the people broke in and tore off the newlyweds' nightshirts to lay bare the places where they had pierced their flesh and drawn blood.

The husband and wife bore neither wounds nor fresh scars. Some called this witchcraft on top of all her other sins; others called it a miracle. One voice even murmured that everyone had been wrong because so many seemed surprised to find moles on Panayiota's chest and back. But no one knew for sure. The people were amazed, and they were afraid.

After that day, people looked her in the eye, and on market day, they took the coins from her hand. No one spat, and the boys made no claims about her. She could even draw water from the same well as everyone else, and others would drink from the dipper she had used.

Soon, Yiorgos bought a donkey, and one morning, the people found his hut empty with the door left open. He must have gone back to his father and taken Panayiota with him.

As they traveled, Yiorgos often stopped to rest. He was still weak from the long wedding night and healing from the wounds where he had pierced the hidden parts of his flesh to paint a stain on the sheets.

account

There came into being a tune that anyone could play. No one knows whether it was written or wrote itself. The virtuosos found it first. They passed it on to their conservatory students. Laymen and children mastered it within a single reading.

Word spread, and soon, anyone who had fingers or a breath took up the tune. As if made of the same matter as the red shoes of legend, the instruments in stores compelled passersby to play. Keyboards and strings were caked with the blood of new musicians who hadn't built up calluses. Playing the tune replaced work: neglected udders burst and mounds of refuse rose in the cities.

After handcuffing each other to vast billiard tables of mahogany to not to reach out, strum, or strike any plangent chord, the authorities ordained the destruction of the tune and every instrument it had infected, except for one copy of the score. That copy was rolled up and archived in a grand piano to wait for scholars and weapons-makers yet unborn.

One convict played as twenty like him hauled what could have been the country's ruin to the highest mountaintop in the middle of the bleakest plain. None came down to claim his pardon.

To this day, men who embark on their last and longest walk will say that they are about to play the peak. Hunters tell of hearing a wind-borne note or two, but no one believes them. The first airplanes—and all since—are routed far around the condemned, resounding place.

engines

Preexistent were the sounds—*vroom, vroom, op, taka, taka, unh*—in rising or descending scales. Birds did not make these sounds, nor did land or sea animals, and none of those sounds echoed the weather.

Yet they came to mind, and they had to be uttered. In places far from one another, little children who had just begun to walk and who would never meet made those sounds as readily as they breathed. Growing older, they did not stop but only vocalized less often in company.

Generations aged and passed away. In late life, each could no longer utter *vroom* or *op* with force from the back of the throat as precisely as before. Nor could they draw *taka taka* from the roofs of their toothless mouths or *unh* from frayed and rheumy sinuses in their final years. The sounds of children and grandchildren could not make up for this loss, which philosophers have struggled to explain without coming to an agreement among themselves.

Some turned instead to reversing that loss and became engineers in doing so. They worked with metal, fire, and what could be brought up from the ground. After countless failures, they arrived at gears and engines. Along with making smoke and steam, their movement could move other objects, especially those with wheels. Above all, their sounds approached the long-sought noises.

Could they be brought closer?

The engineers brought forth trains, automobiles, and outboard motors. All were foretold by the distant echo of past voices. The lexicon expanded with the jackhammer, the hydraulic brake, and the jet engines with their occasional *boom* across the sound barrier. The dreams of the old were fulfilled, and they now dreamed about the new added works that surrounded them. The young made these new noises with vigor.

Generations reached the end of their days without knowing another path. The last generations to walk had long since perished, but new generations were amazed when the liquids and stones from the earth grew harder to find or gave out altogether. Churnings and whines once ubiquitous as birdsong grew less common and quieter. Soon, they disappeared. Trains' *taka taka* continued for a while longer; some say they still move in a far land.

The old knew a loss once confined to letters and works of history. Some wondered if that loss had never receded but only been masked. Along with some engineers, they turned to addressing the questions that had eluded other times, and even in the absence of agreement, they persisted.

The young men and women uttered the sounds that now came from nowhere else, as many children did with toys carved in the shape of vehicles they had seen in a museum.

Surviving engines, in their minds, were the sounds.

Vroom.

one foot

Sheila knows the rule. One foot on the floor or the ground. This applies generally like gravity, the drinking age, or the certainty that a quadratic equation must equal zero no matter what turns and twists it takes through bracketed xs and ys. One foot. The rule applies specifically to pool as her father explained at the basement table. It applies to throwing a softball from short to first as her coach insisted.

She leans back onto her bed, draws up one leg, and lists more applications. During oboe practice, she must keep her spine and diaphragm aligned and tap time—quietly—on the floor. Once, after practicing for hours, both of her feet fell asleep, and blood pooled in her calves. She brought up her legs, but Mr. Reichling walked over and flicked a baton against her thigh.

He said, sotto voce, "Sitting that way was fine for primitive people but not for a white classical musician."

She brought her feet down and tried to keep up with the strings and the pianist. Brahms couldn't be disrupted, even from second chair. She missed a few notes, swallowing tears and draining her sinuses.

She switched legs and arched her back.

When she was seven and said she didn't need naps, she fell asleep in the afternoon on her bed, this bed. The day after she got her tonsils removed, she fell asleep on the couch. But that wasn't a nap. One foot stayed on the floor; a heel wedged itself into the shag carpet. Splitting hairs like that, she could become a lawyer. Perhaps. The SAT and LSAT are still to come.

She tenses her leg and shoulder muscles until they threaten to break out of her skin. Only one example is left, but she wants to go on listing like the way she did once on a history exam. When the hour was over, she had cataloged fifteen causes of the Civil War. Ten were enough for an A, but she had found a rhythm and couldn't stop.

But only one item remains: men and women.

When her parents watched Dick Van Dyke before she was born, they pointed out how Rob and Laurie Petrie kept a foot on the floor even when they sat on their own double beds as the censors had prescribed.

"That may not have been a bad idea," her mother said. "Maybe we should have tried that a little more often." She would always add the same advice. "It's too late for us, Sheila, but that might be a good idea for when you have a boy over here. It will help you set the right tone."

She knows the rule in her muscles and joints even if it doesn't come to mind. She shifts her weight. For a moment, she keeps both feet down before bringing one up again to the air and then the bed.

Above her, the boy thrusts, trying to get the rhythm that was momentarily broken back. He doesn't ask about the exam, the SAT, throwing from short, or the oboe. Neither did the boy last week or the others.

Once he restores the rhythm, her foot takes it up, tapping andante. The tapping travels through the floorboards and the walls but diminishes on the way to the basement. It registers with her parents as familiar and comforting as when she keeps time, sight-reading a new score.

appellative

The Man of the Highly Common Name is always and everywhere reminded of who he is.

While making a dinner reservation or a medical appointment—and not to mention checking into a hotel room—he braces himself for the pause in conversation, the doubting looks, and the tired jokes. He keeps the explanations and ripostes in mind as others do not. Plane travel means allowing extra time at the airport to prove he is not some other bearer of the Highly Common Name, one—presumably more than one—who stands out from the crowd by way of crime. He avoids jobs in public relations and other types of sales.

By definition, the Man of the Highly Common Name is not alone in his dilemma. He has confirmed this by leafing through telephone directories in other cities. Conducting vanity searches with major and minor engines, he finds thousands of pages that include his name and those who share it: a retired football player, a knife maker, a Sanskrit scholar, a physicist, etc. None are himself, though he often feels spread thin.

Yet not all of his namesakes are distant strangers. He is, in fact, Highly Common Name Jr. Raised in a small town, his father remembers times before television, before irony and sandwiches made it on an industrial scale. Highly Common Name, Sr. meant no harm by naming his son after himself.

Fond of his father and admittedly slothful in matters of paperwork, the Man of the Highly Common Name declines to change his name.

He explores other means of addressing his dilemma, such as sleeping as long and as often as he can. He is good at this, and it is free. But he must go to work some time, and even to the deepest recesses of sleep come dreams that reenact his waking life.

The Man of the Highly Common Name attempts to drink until he can no longer remember that name but instead confirms his suspicions: he possesses an impeccable memory, and he suffers numerous hangovers.

Other drugs lie out of reach. Making discreet inquiries of people who know others who could meet his needs, the Man of the Highly Common Name finds that he must prove his good faith. He shows his checkbook, credit cards, new and old utility bills, driver's license, and passport. They provoke one response: "Nobody will believe that. They'll think you're a narc."

Only then, too late to help him obtain controlled substances, does the Man of the Highly Common Name acquire nicknames, street names, and noms de plume. Some are given by others, but most he gives himself as others send themselves flowers at the office. No one has a bigger collection; no one needs them more. These nicknames take on a weight, accreting like tiles that made armor before the Iron Age. They still prove inadequate. If his given name affords no more than a baggy fit over the specifics of his being, those additions cover only a small portion of those contours, and daylight is between them.

His troubles are too great to bear alone. The Man of the Highly Common Name seeks company. He makes friends among those with rare names that are foreign and hard to spell, as a giant may befriend a dwarf. Those friends' problems are not his problems. Their names have been butchered by gym teachers, cut short on standardized forms, and made the raw material of taunts and puns. Those friends would prefer to be him as he would prefer to be them.

Over time, they have little to talk about besides who is the giant and who is the dwarf. Friends drift apart.

The Man of the Highly Common Name decides to think bigger. He goes to distant lands while on sabbatical. Instead of being known by everyone, he is now known by no one.

While introducing himself in several destinations, he hears, "So, you are a typical person from your country." Some have their photographs taken with him.

Home again, the Man of the Highly Common Name reads as he has never read before. Book after book asks him questions other than what people call him, and he comes to understand why pages have been called talking leaves. He does not hear voices or hallucinate; he only reads.

Having read, the Man of the Highly Common Name takes long walks out of town. Depending on his mood, he speaks and sometimes sings to livestock and wild creatures. Depending on their mood, they answer in their own ways or keep still. They ask no questions.

Needing rest, the Man of the Highly Common Name learns to sit quietly in a room alone. Some have given labels to this practice and classified its varieties, but he has lost his appetite for designations. He lets the seconds and the hours wash over him. The hull of addressing and being addressed softens and falls away.

He unfurls, taking root and nourishment.

preliminary

The candidate continued learning about his potential workplace even as he approached the main entrance.

Sitting at a bench and wearing a company ID with its large and famous logo, a woman of late middle age smoked a cigarette without any stealth or shame that was expected in most places. Human frailty was understood here.

As it was the summer of the seventeenth year, cicadas bumbled and crawled above ground, and one landed in front of the woman's foot. She stomped once with her stiletto and missed, but she drove the insect under the bench. From there, it moved toward a tree. The woman hunched, stretched a leg under the bench, and resumed kicking. She came closer with each attempt. Her lipstick turned upward into something like a smile.

There were plenty of other places to work and plenty of other people to work with. This place, however, could be home.

interurban

eurail

Living on next to nothing, like a bromeliad, I traveled Europe on trains among other students. I slept on overnight routes to save money on lodging and drank countless liters of water from ribbed plastic bottles. What came from the restroom faucets wasn't potable. Off the train, I saw enough of the continent to recall a detail or nod among similarly traveled peers who might be in a position to offer me work or sex.

Between Thessaloniki and Istanbul, I met the only obnoxious Canadian in captivity. When I returned from the floor-level latrine, he was sitting in my compartment in place of the Greek whose earphones had spilled out Led Zeppelin. Before I could slide the door closed and take refuge behind *The Herald Tribune*, he looked straight at me.

"Hi. You speak English, don't you?"

I nodded but didn't get to elaborate.

"Great. You looked like you did. I hope you don't mind that I put your backpack up in the rack. I might have done you a favor though. It's heavy, and you're not a very big guy."

He leaned across the compartment to set my water bottle upright—the backpack might have knocked it over on the way up—then lowered into his seat. My hopes of catching up on the baseball scores rose and then fell as he raised the window and lit a Rothmans.

"I'm sorry. I should have introduced myself."

I insisted there was no need, but the protest failed.

"I am Jack DuMonde. That's French for *of the world*—the DuMonde part, not the Jack part. I come to Europe about once a year."

He pronounced *about* as *a boat*. I could only wonder why he had not been kept in his home and native land as a cautionary example for both young citizens and immigrants seeking to fit in: this was how *not* to be a Canadian.

Jack took a deep puff and resumed. "Where are you going?"

"Istanbul. I'm going to see the Hagia Sophia."

"It's a shame how the government has let it get run down, but you should still see it. I hope that's not all you see though." He leaned forward as if to take me by the shoulders and could have if I hadn't shrunk back. "Listen. We're both men. There are things we can talk about." We were alone, but he still lowered his voice. "You've got to go to a little district on the Asian side called Iti Buçuk. Suck indeed, let me tell you. It's amazing what you can get for only a few dollars." He took a breath before continuing. "I know I'm going on a bit. It's an occupational hazard when you're in communications. Do you know anything about the field?"

I felt cornered. "Yes but not very much."

He took my words for fascination. Through fields, terraced hills, and interchangeable villages, I learned about ratings, market shares, and quarterly earnings. Syndication rights and production values. What exactly he communicated did not come up. The outrageous demands of advertisers and the lack of good restaurants on his stretch of Yonge Street did though. Expense account meals on the road made up for it.

Several stops later, as we passed one of the last minarets in Greece, Jack asked what I did. He took note, briefly, and said that one of his staff had a background in international relations like me. The young man could never quite make the transition from academic concepts to the practical realm of completing assignments. He would have to be let go after Jack returned to Toronto.

His last cigarette took us from the arid foothills to the swamps of Thrace. He opened the window and tossed out the butt. "I've never seen the need for those signs. 'It is dangerous to lean out.' Of course, it's dangerous to lean out. How stupid do they think people are?"

"It can't be too dangerous," I said. "Unless you climb up on something, you can't get very far out."

There was a chance, however small, that he would try, and I did not want to discourage him. It was a long way to Istanbul.

At the last stop on the Greek side, the government flexed its border control muscles to impress the Turks, inspecting passports in the compartments to hold up the train. For two hours, we had the opportunity to patronize the station shop, stocked with feta and fried chickpeas, or stand in the morning's chill. Along the tracks, an English student complained—at first to the uncomprehending conductors but then to no one in particular—that his girlfriend was sick. Another American, a blonde in khaki shorts, discussed her plan to travel alone in the Anatolian outback. Neither had a spare seat to offer.

When I boarded for the short trip to the Turkish side, where the government would flex its border control muscles to impress the Greeks, Jack had not moved except to fold my newspaper inside out and open the window, admitting a cloud of mosquitoes.

He swatted one into a bloody paste on his forearm. "Damned mosquitoes. Maybe I should say damned kounoupia. That's what the Greeks call them." He stretched out the word a second time. "Kou-nou-pia. I don't know what they're called in Turkish."

A rose by any other name though. The next one he fed might be malarial.

I still had a long way to Istanbul, and the delay on the Turkish side was supposedly four hours. Now and then, a German would have to open their bags and sometimes a Canadian but only after all the Americans' bags were checked. The occasional detained Yank kept the arms sales forthcoming and muted official complaints about Cyprus. The others were for practice.

This reminded me of something I had forgotten. I nearly forgot again as Jack spoke. "Say, would you mind watching my things for a minute? I must have gotten a bad piece of moussaka. I'm nearly bent in two."

Outside my window, fields of stooped farmers and grazing goats were luxurious with silence. If my books could have spoken, they would have shouted. Besides Hobbes, I was reviewing Thucydides to prepare for a fall seminar and kept returning to the Melian dialogue. The Athenians offered the Melians a choice between peaceful surrender and annihilation as, in the world, the strong do what they can, and the weak suffer what they must. People may choose to be one or the other, but the justice of their cause did not matter. For several hours, I had made the wrong choice. Choosing again, I opened my backpack and Jack's duffel bag.

When he came back, much relieved, we discussed the hole in the ozone layer, our favorite sites in Milan, and why the Canadians and Brits spelled *favorite* with a *u*. After we turned over our passports for examination, Jack mentioned where he was going to stay and suggested I get a room there.

I refolded my newspaper as the gendarmes returned to our compartment.

One asked the inevitable question. "American?"

I nodded.

"Luggage, please."

I pointed to the backpack and motioned for help. The taller officer took one end of the frame, and together, we brought it down.

Bored, I watched him work through the assorted packs and pouches. No Fourth Amendment protected me from his search, and no gloves protected him from three weeks of soiled clothes.

He zipped the backpack, lifted it without my help, and thanked me for my cooperation.

His colleague turned to Jack. "American?"

"No, Canadian."

The gendarme paused and then stated, "Luggage, please."

Jack brought down the duffel bag and opened it so quickly that the zipper shrieked.

The gendarme casually fingered the clothing but then stopped, pulling out a plastic bag. "What is this?"

"I don't know. I've never seen it before."

The taller officer blocked the door.

"Come with us, please."

The officers took him by either arm; the larger carried his duffel bag. As they elbowed the door open and walked out, Jack looked over his shoulder. I saw confusion and fear.

My journey with him, and with some of Amsterdam's finer hashish, was done. I took out Thucydides and lit a Dunhill to ward off the kounoupia.

Jack's choice of lodging, a guest house on the European side with Western toilets, turned out to be a bargain, though prices in Iti Buçuk had risen since his last visit. For two days, I walked in and out of domed wonders, drank glass after small glass of tea with rug and leather merchants, and ate enough doughy rings of simit to have sleeved an arm in them.

*

None of this would matter if I had never seen him again, but after a decade, in which I had learned to live on tenure and the smoke and mirrors of a theory on Third World politics, he appeared to me in Houston.

Preparing to present a paper that opposed foreign aid, I surfed the channels in my hotel room and came across a newscast mentioning a book, among other things, on Turkish prisons—a latter-day *Midnight Express*. In her professionally flat voice, the interviewer introduced, "Our guest this morning is author Jack DuMonde."

His face was still round, if more wrinkled, and words still streamed from it, but they were now *arrest* and *imprisonment* instead of *ratings* and *brothels*. He called his sentence more fortunate than his release. In his heart, he had forgiven whoever had planted the drugs and now wanted to express his thanks. He'd had the opportunity to become a Christian, taking the road to Damascus in the exercise yard at the rate of thirty minutes a week. The newsreader could stomach this no more than I could and went to break, noting that his book was moving up *The New York Times* bestseller list.

I mashed the power button and tossed the remote onto the bed. I had only needed to be rid of the man for a few hours to get some peace, quiet, and maybe a little sleep. Now, I would have to hide from him and his gratitude in my own country, and if he wrote anything like the way he talked, there would be more books to come.

On my way out, I had a shot from the bottle of single malt on my nightstand. I needed to steady my nerves for my presentation. But it did nothing to dull an old craving that had now returned. For all the money I spent and all the trouble I went through, I barely made a dent in that hash.

I haven't found any better.

el vato

I was first mistaken for El Vato before I even knew who he was. Buying coffee and beans in Cholula, I approached the counter with the goods in one hand and dug for money in my rucksack with the other. As I found Sor Juana Inés de la Cruz looking up repeatedly from a stack of bills, the clerk spoke up in the region's intelligible Spanish.

"Stop! Take your hand out of the bag slowly and drop both bags. Good. Now raise your hands."

I looked up to find the clerk aiming a nine-millimeter at my chest. I had nothing else to do but wonder how many rounds the clip held before I stammered the most important words in any language. "No me mate." *Don't kill me.* I should have said *mates,* the familiar form, but I found a certain inequality in our relationship.

At least the clerk didn't correct my usage. "Stay where you are," he said, walking around the counter and remembering to click off the safety. "You may be El Vato everywhere else, but in my store, you are just another motherless pig."

"No soy él," I said a little above a whisper. *I am not him.*

"So, this is the man who is capable of anything. How do you feel now, pistolero?"

I felt irritated on the behalf of the man I wasn't—not that I was fond of him at the moment. "Listen, I am not the man you are talking about. Search my pockets. Look anywhere you want."

He worked through the groceries and the rucksack, and he frisked me as quickly as possible to avoid looking like a maricón. He held the picture page of my US passport up to my face. "This could be worth some money if you ever want to lose it."

He pointed to the wall behind me with his pistol, and I cringed before he spoke. "Okay. You're not him. Turn around." I saw the poster. "That's the man we're looking for. He has killed many, and there is a price on his head. Be careful. You look like brothers."

Grateful for my life, I added two cans of jalapeños and a box of Gamesa wafers to my purchase.

*

Don Ramiro, the foreman of my field crew, explained El Vato. "El Vato," he intoned, "is he with whom one does not play. He kills men the way we shovel dirt. It is his work."

I asked about the resemblance.

He agreed.

I asked why he had never said anything.

"At first, I didn't know. If you weren't him, I didn't want to give offense. If you were, I wanted to live."

*

A week later, buying rice and cheese in Puebla, I left my rucksack at the dig site and carried only my wallet and passport. At the counter, I kept my empty hands in front of me and hooked the plastic bags over one arm. I pivoted to give the clerk a view of my back pocket and reached for my money slowly. Another copy of the poster faced me. I pointed to it and explained. "No soy él." I am not him.

The clerk gave me my change and smiled. "Perhaps you are not him. Perhaps you are. It doesn't matter." He tapped his belt holster that had a banker's special with a checkered wood handle, perhaps .30 caliber.

Cautious and grateful again, I bought a bottle of mineral water for the drive back and took an extra copy of the poster to display at the site.

*

At five-three, I didn't cut the figure of a pistolero, but the poster listed El Vato at 1.67 meters and fifty-eight kilos. Nor did I look Mexican. Neither did El Vato. It was believed that his father was a blond Galician and his mother a Lebanese who had found it advisable to leave Mexico City.

Most accounts called her bruja, a witch. After her first two children, both monsters, died hours after birth, she vowed that her next child's life would embody her vengeance on the world and on the God who had taken his brothers.

She raised him accordingly. His first words were a curse—no one agreed on the exact words—and his first toy was a stick he used to club iguanas for meat and for sport. At the movies, he learned to cheer on the villain gunning for Pedro Infante or Vicente Fernández that week. Any religion he had involved lighting candles and offering rum and chickens to the gods worshipped by the Veracruz mulattoes.

The fights, robberies, violations, and killings progressed like grade levels. At the age of seventeen, he was wanted in three states. In the fifteen years since, a hundred deaths had been attributed to him. Others might have involved him, but the witnesses grew reluctant or disappeared.

Even his amusements caused fear. El Vato halved oranges by throwing a knife, and he took target practice by shooting beer bottles from drinkers' hands. In a good mood—having hit no one by mistake and missing no one he aimed for—he would buy a round to replace what was spilled, and everyone drank whether they were thirsty or not.

As facts were transposed in retelling, El Vato, raised to bear vengeance against the Creator, was often called the wrath of God. After one of his attacks, whole towns repented. Evangelicals returned to Catholicism; Catholics became Evangelicals. Mormons learned to drink.

*

My relations with the area's shopkeepers proceeded cautiously but with courtesy. They did not take for granted my untested capacity for violence or my demonstrated capacity for impulse buying.

Still, I was watched on the streets and in the plazas. Conversations paused mid-sentence—mid-word even—as those who passed me averted their eyes. Parents drew their children close.

Hoping a change of appearance would help, I studied the poster to differ from it. As El Vato was clean-shaven, I let my beard grow out.

I asked Don Ramiro what he thought of my effort.

"I think," he said, "that you look like El Vato with a beard and mustache."

*

Visiting a colleague in Morelos, I stopped for gas and a newspaper. Walking back to the truck with my change, I heard a hollow pop. A windowpane broke somewhere behind me, and several voices shouted at once. I could still make out what each said.

"Get down!"

"Danger!"

A woman said, "They are going to kill him."

After another hollow pop, the shouts made sense.

I ran behind the truck, and another bullet skimmed the rear fender.

I edged into the cab and looked back. Fifty or sixty meters behind me, a pair of federales shouldered their rifles, lowered them, and drove away from Morelos after seeing my face. I did not even ask not to be killed.

Before driving away, I read the paper and learned that El Vato had held up a liquor store in Mexico City. He was reportedly headed west. I sat for several more minutes as the afternoon rain started and stopped before pulling out. Customers came out from the gas station and the restaurant, and the paleta vendor stepped out from behind his chilly cart. Unable to see everyone, I stopped and shouted out the window. "No me maten!"

The onlookers smiled, for lack of anything else to do. There was a certain inequality at work. They had just seen me ward off two federales who would rather retreat than take a chance on my returning fire. Some of their colleagues, I learned later, had not been so cautious.

*

At my insistence, my field crew and I stayed in all weekend and discussed plans for my second season of excavation if I lived that long. One afternoon, while I napped, my colleague went out and had a T-shirt made for me. The front read, "No soy él," and the back read, "No me maten, por favor."

I put on the shirt for the trip back to Cholula, and on the way, I heard radio reports of El Vato in my clothing. He must have heard the same reports, and their caveat that the identification was not positive. Within days, he was seen wearing the same shirt in Oaxaca, where I had never been.

As the price on his head rose, my face and clothing lost their credibility. If I was going to be shot at anyway, I had to return fire. I started carrying a nine-millimeter with two spare clips and took target practice on fence posts and an occasional scorpion.

*

The ground hardened from lack of rain and only grudgingly yielded its meters to the excavation. One afternoon in the last week of the season, I gave in to temptation and started digging with the blade of the claw hammer. Dirt flew quickly until I was reminded why we were taught not to dig with a blade.

One blow ended with a crack, and the shock traveled up my arm. The dust opened to an arc of a skull that had lain centuries before being fractured.

I gathered the bone chips into a plastic bag, unearthed the rest of the skull—ruined with the same tool in Mexico City or as my own would be if a civic-minded bullet struck— and emptied it like an eggshell. I hyperventilated and then vomited. I didn't go for drinks with the crew that night and turned off my bedroom light before undressing.

*

At the season's end, I drove north through Coahuila, hugged the Gulf Coast, and heard more radio reports of the occasional sightings of El Vato or me, though the situation wasn't without its advantages. I wasn't allowed to pay for gas or food.

In Matamoros, I stopped for lunch before crossing the border into Brownsville. With US Customs ahead, there was no telling when I would eat again.

The worst, though, had to be over. I put on my disclaimer T-shirt to start a conversation with friends in Corpus Christi that night.

After finding a restaurant with outside seating and convincing a shoeshine boy that my hiking boots didn't need a polish, I looked across a few empty tables and saw my putative twin, sitting behind a clutch of empty beer bottles and looking more drawn than the posters had shown him. I hadn't enjoyed the best of summers myself.

He looked up and spoke without hesitation. "So, it's you I've been hearing about. It's you who have made the police come out in force and have kept me from having a good night's sleep."

I swallowed hard and, knowing I was being listened to, said, "That's funny. That's what I was going to tell you."

He sat up slowly, with too much effort, and spoke again. "I've had enough of your interference. You are not going to bother me anymore."

The table and bottles hid most of his body, but the rolling of his shoulders meant he was drawing. Had he been sober, I would have died where I sat. Instead, I put two rounds in his chest. He squeezed off several high, wild shots before falling over.

I would have preferred to eat at the table but felt compelled to settle for a beer and a sandwich to go. Under the circumstances, I laid large tips on both tables.

*

The second season of excavation is underway but, like the first, is going too slowly. As the man who killed El Vato, I receive visitors almost daily and letters constantly. The handwriting is from people who are seldom called upon to write, and I am obliged to honor their effort with a reply.

On the other hand, some believe El Vato gunned down his assailant or survived the attack. To them, I am he. I am consequently invited to weddings, baptisms, and occasionally a funeral. Attending some events, I feel safe as the police share my view of last year's gunfight. To others, I send only regrets.

My traveling, though, is limited. Don Ramiro tells me that if I venture into the southern states, where the women are forward, I will be deluged with marriage proposals or just propositions and ignoring them would only bring me more attention.

In my capacities as El Vato and his killer, I lose a day of work every week and most of my free time. The crew is good, but the ground is hard, and the meters yield slowly.

fighting words

I could pass if I wanted to. Nobody followed me around in a store, and I had only been pulled over for speeding.

I could go through Harlem and DC, along with Houston's Fifth Ward and most of Atlanta, without hearing a panhandler say, "Why won't you help out another brother?" then call me *oreo* or *bougie* when I keep walking. I had been mistaken for Jewish and Lebanese, and once somebody thought I was Armenian. That still made me trip. At the airport in Las Vegas, a high roller whose comped drinks hadn't worn off asked, "What are you?" After I explained, he thanked me for my time and shook my hand—I gave him credit for that—but he held something back from his grip.

That was why it threw people off sometimes when I went down the street humming, "Lift Every Voice and Sing." But I didn't need the Nation of Islam bowtie and bean pie posse to tell me who I am. I got my one drop and then some.

Exactly how a blue-black man born in Holly Springs, Mississippi ended up marrying a white woman in the 1920s never got explained to me, but they stayed together until she passed on before I was born. Great-Granddad James—we usually left out the *great*—didn't join her until I was in college. He was getting tired by the time I finished high school, but when I walked across the stage at graduation, he had said, "Hoo! Look at the big man!" loud enough for the people on the opposite bleachers to hear.

We'd gotten to do a lot up to that point since he was the only grandfather I had. Dad's dad was killed in World War II, and Mom's dad had fallen into a bottle somewhere. Nobody had heard from him since the sixties. Granddad James took me into the big AME Church on 79th Street in Chicago enough that I still get my nose out of joint just thinking about the crowds that just think of gospel choirs as a side dish for their Sunday brunch. Once, Granddad James even took me along to see Muddy Waters—*Mr. Morganfield* or *sir* as I was to call him—after the King Bee had packed up his guitar and moved to Western Springs in the suburbs. They were some kind of shirttail relation, which made me one too. *Damn.* Mr. Morganfield said, "Boy looks like Charlie Patton."

Mostly, I would go over to Granddad James' house while he cooked. We had plenty of time to talk. He fried up pork chops until I could have used them to resole his Stacey Adams shoes. "I've seen what trichinosis can do to a man," he had told me.

Otherwise, he knew what he was doing. I begged like a dog for his sweet potato pie, and the first vegetable I ever willingly ate was his collard greens. When I was about six, I didn't have my words right and called them coloreds, and he laughed before setting me straight so that I wouldn't get into any drama somewhere else.

I couldn't go the distance to chitlins, though, even before I dissected a fetal pig in high school biology. I'd only dare him, saying, "You're not going to eat that," and he would say right back, "You just watch me, boy." I did, and he did. Only toward the end did he say, "That ain't for everybody. You get a taste for it early, or you don't get it at all. Was a damn sight better than going to bed hungry every night."

*

It wasn't exactly clear why I was thinking about this in the bar at Chicago Union Station while I waited to take a less crowded train home. There was no telling what I could start thinking about after I missed lunch for a meeting with nothing since but one Manhattan and most of a second. They went down easy enough, and I could pretend the maraschino cherry was food.

Manhattan the Third or something close enough, Maker's Mark, straight up took its place on a coaster in front of me, and I let the drink sit for now. I was already set up proper. I had forgotten to bring anything to read—it had been that kind of day from the start—but going to the newsstand could cost me my seat. This left the television that was turned to news or what somebody decided was news: an earthquake in Asia, famine in Ethiopia, stocks that most people didn't own, and crimes done to or by the Black community. Sports showed a pitchout by a Cubs reliever who loaded the bases. The next Astros batter got a grand slam.

The drinker a couple of stools away, who looked about sixty and had been there when I arrived, was reloading with a fresh Old Style. He offered an assessment that network color commentators could only dream of giving. "That pitcher must have balls the size of peas."

Not looking to join the conversation, I held back a laugh.

"I don't know," said a younger man to his right, who had also been there from the first. "That batter's been on a tear lately, and the next guy was in a slump."

"Hell of a way to break out of it."

"Yeah."

The broadcast moved on. Without another disaster or a baby animal at the Brookfield Zoo, the producers scraped the bottom of the barrel and found a science item: new evidence that humans were descended from a handful of women in East Africa.

"You feel African?" asked the older man.

"Not today," said his young new friend, his partner. "If I did, I might be running with a football and getting a couple million dollars."

"Or food stamps and a welfare check."

This wasn't the time or place to school my bar mates on the welfare reforms of the nineties and the origin of food stamps as a farm subsidy. I didn't have the details chapter and verse, and they didn't look like they would spend their Wednesday evening looking them up online. I'm not proud of it, but I have a prejudice or two of my own.

All I needed to do was catch a train, and I was taking tomorrow off for a parent-teacher conference. I gripped the rocks glass and thought about taking a sip but didn't.

"They can run like hell though," the younger man said.

"Put a stolen chicken under their arms, you'll see how fast they can really run."

The partner chortled once and turned thoughtful in a half-drunken way. "But that's a hell of a thing. You ever wonder why they can do that?"

"I don't think. I *know*," said the commentator. "A lot of things make them different."

Like some people collected old-school lawn jockeys and segregated water fountain signs, I liked to count how many knuckleheaded claims in Column A would match the knuckleheaded claims I'd heard before in Column B.

"They're put together different for jungle skills like outrunning a lion."

Check. Lions lived on savannas and not in rain forests. Not even Carl Lewis in his prime could have outrun a motivated lion.

"That's why they've got an extra bone in their foot." Check. "And their backbones slide in some kind of way. That's why they can dance like that." Check. Possibly check again. The part about rhythm was implied.

"But they sure don't read or write good," the partner said. "Why's that?"

"Reading and writing, my friend, are not exactly jungle skills. That's why those people are fast instead of smart." Still not joining in, I didn't bring up my Richard Wright first editions and my signed copy of *Invisible Man*. Or the biography of Pushkin, who was Black like me.

"But you take anything physical, and they're all over it when they feel like it."

"That goes back to their jungle equipment and how they handle the heat," said the aging expert in human variation. "They don't sweat. They secrete a kind of oil."

No check. This was a new one.

"You're kidding."

"No. When I was growing up, my doctor told me about it."

"But they're still human."

"Hell, you can call a horse human if you want to."

It probably wouldn't have helped to whinny or neigh, pretending to be Mr. Ed in a jacket and tie, but that crossed my mind. Maybe I should have.

"Don't get me wrong," the partner said. "I don't like them either." He then spat out the word, the one everybody knows and rhymes with trigger when people pronounce the *r*. I don't use it, and I didn't like it when the young people did, taking the *r* off when they wanted to sound street smart or were just acting ignorant, degrading themselves like that. Looking the way I do, though, I have to hold my tongue. My opinion might not carry a lot of weight.

The man caught himself and gave the room a once-over before relaxing in a way that meant *You can say that word here*. He added, "But they're more or less like us."

"That's where you're wrong, my friend. It's like that doctor told me. They're a lower breed, and it's time we stopped treating them like they weren't."

There was a lull in the conversation. This was the time and place. After picking a few words, I joined in. "Excuse me, sir. Your comments are becoming offensive."

"Oh, Christ," the commentator said. He looked me over with eyes that couldn't quite focus. "Are you one of those ACLU civil rights people who go around looking to stand up for principles?" He ended the word *principles* with a *sh* sound, the beer working on him. I didn't have a chance to answer the question. "It's not like you're one of them."

"Sir, I *am* one of them."

He paused. "Then how come you're so articulate?"

I never knew when that word was going to come up but always knew how. *Articulate* came with the unspoken reservation "for one of them."

I didn't answer the question but thought of the Dunbar poem Granddad James had shown me. I was wearing the mask, more than I had to at the moment, but a whole lot less than Granddad James had to wear it every damned day of his life. "Sir, if you could only be considerate, I would appreciate it."

"You don't have to listen."

At this point, a friend could have said, "Take it easy," called him by his first name, and put a hand on his shoulder, buying me time to think.

"Sir, this is a public place, and you're nearby. It's hard not to listen."

I had tried to give him a graceful way out, but I had apparently failed. The man tensed up like he was cornered. "Then listen to this," he said, raising his voice. People were watching now. "I am going to say whatever the hell I want, and there's not a goddamned thing you can do about it." He added the word.

It hung in the air like a puff of foul smoke.

Now I tensed up, backed into a corner of my own. In some circles, the African American male has a reputation for poor impulse control, but no one sees the impulses we *do* control. I pushed down a few of those impulses before giving in to one.

The mask came off.

I splashed the man with my drink.

"Motherfucker," he slurred and rose to his feet. I didn't draw back right away because I didn't believe what he was doing. He caught my jaw with most of a right hook. I gripped the bar to keep from falling and then stood up.

I didn't want this. Not the embarrassment. Not the damage to my suit. Not the disruption of my evening. None of it. I backed up, but he kept coming.

I didn't back up again. I blocked his next punch and tagged him in the ribs. We stood there, teeing off on each other until we ran out of breath. We clinched and worked in a shot here and there: one more fight between out-of-shape men. Neither of us would step off.

I heard the barmaid shout and make a phone call. Comments circled around the bar but not for long.

Two officers showed up fast. Around this time of day, they wouldn't have much else to do besides rattle the benches in the Great Hall to keep the homeless awake. One policeman pulled my hands behind my back and handcuffed me before the other could restrain his suspect, who got in one more punch.

I don't know what the other officer did with his man. Mine, a brown-skinned man who was a few years older than me, walked me through the station and up the stairs to Canal Street.

He didn't ask me any questions or read me my rights; so far, I wasn't formally under arrest. I watched the traffic and tried to read his expression but couldn't. I stood there, wondering why the CPD hatband was a black-and-white checkerboard.

As a patrol car pulled up, I asked, "Do you know what happened?"

He shook his head without meeting my eyes. He'd probably had his fill of conversations like this. I hadn't.

I told him what he called me.

Now the officer looked me over, searching my features for something like his own. He didn't offer any validation, but to his credit, he didn't laugh at me either.

"I *am* one," I said as the patrol car pulled up.

He opened the front door and put my briefcase in the passenger side. Then he opened the back door for me.

"You are now, my brother," he said. He placed his right hand on top of my head to protect it from the door frame and roof, guiding me into the back seat with something like tenderness.

quarter

I don't know what her name is, so I think of her according to
what she says. Quarter is in the house, in the wider sense of
the word that includes the S-2 bus southbound on 16th Street.
This means I don't have to check my watch or scam off
someone else's before going back to the new book on the
disappearance of the Anasazi. I know what time it is: between
8:49 and 8:52 Eastern Time—and we're just north of Newton
Street, headed toward the White House.

In this window of time, Quarter boards and drops her
coins in the fare box. Some of the bus drivers just say what
they would to anyone else, which ranges from "Have a blessed
morning" to nothing at all, just a quick glance at her money
before popping the trap door and sending the change to its
afterlife in the floor safe.

Others have more to say. The tones echo the preaching
they must have heard growing up. The dashboard sermonette
goes from "Act right now" to "I want you to leave those people
alone today." Once, a driver turned his post into a pup-tent
revival and issued a dire warning of Metrobus damnation.
"Don't make me put you out at the next stop, and I will if you
get unruly." I don't know if she followed instructions that day.
I went back to reading an article on a recent Zapotec
excavation.

In my experience though, one of the great phrases to use
in writing an after-dinner speech is—whatever the drivers
say—Quarter just goes on with her own digging. The fare

apparently taps out her cash reserves, and she works the bus like a candidate working a room of campaign contributors in a movie directed by David Lynch. She poses the same question from the front of the bus to the back and then toward the front again, a land-based salmon going upstream against the passengers who have since boarded and stand in the aisles.

The question being: do you have quarter?

No *a* before the noun. The words ring in a breathy East Asian accent. The roundness of her face makes me think Korean or northern Chinese. They don't, in fact, all look alike. I paid off my master's degree in archaeology, which now mostly gave me things to read about on the bus and a couple of other detours that didn't pay the bills, while helping a Texan with damage control when he'd said as much. My first task was coaching him on when—almost always these days— a speaker shouldn't call other groups of people *they*.

Wherever she's from, the English, as a lot of the world calls it, is not her first language. The dropped *a* shows that. That much stays with me from my time teaching English as a second language before coming over to the dark side and making a living.

How dark? There's no way to measure these things.

How much of a living? Not enough to afford a decent car and parking, but there is hope: I work for men who have them.

I don't know how Quarter fits into the world. Hell, I don't know how I do. But she looks too old to be a smart-ass kid messing with the grown-ups, too clean and well-fed to be homeless or an addict, and far too young to be someone

93

broken down and landing hard in her final years. She stands up straight, and she has better skin than I do after the last few years of long hours and fast food. Dressed in a plain blouse and slacks, she looks too casually dressed for a lot of jobs, unless this is her job. I have a hard time imagining how she spends the rest of her day or where she goes home at night.

Quarter's progress continues. Sometimes, a little dog in my mind salivates at the bell of her words. Not with desire. Instead, the little dog drools with questions. What if she knows English perfectly well, accent or no, and means damned well to drop the *a*? What if she knows exactly what she is doing and is engaged in an anthropological field study to see how the natives react? Or what if she is an actress, preparing for a role? Most theaters in the District never get on C-SPAN.

The guesses give way to facts as she begs down the rows. "Do you have quarter?"

It would be one hell of a performance: the performer is submerged in the part, and the actor's identity is subsumed in the role. If she is studying the rest of us, her information gathering would be as flawless as if Margaret Mead had herself been Samoan.

But no actor would rehearse a single line for a year. No anthropologist would need to observe the same population so many times.

All that's left is the obvious: Quarter is not quite right.

Could she be Mongoloid in both senses?

Scratch that. That phrase couldn't even make it into the first draft of a speech. What is the clinical term these days?

Down syndrome or some other diagnosis? *Developmentally disabled* was the phrase a few years ago. Now it's *developmentally challenged*, though *challenge* sounds like something people can turn down instead of something they're stuck with. I've seen more than one candidate lose an endorsement by muffing a choice of words.

There is the outside chance that she is just someone in the normal range of smarts, as if that isn't disappointing enough, who hasn't been treated for obsessive-compulsive disorder. She performs the same ritual over and over.

But the intensity is missing, and I'll be damned if there isn't even a certain grace to it. She slowly places a little of her weight on the handrail, and each time, she asks, "Do you have quarter?"

When the rookies, who haven't cut through her accent, ask her to repeat herself, she keeps her voice low and says only, "Quarter."

This is not the premedication spaz I went through, checking the alarm four or five times a night before going to bed and waking up two or three times again to check the alarm several more times. Not like the way I make sure the apartment door is locked before leaving in the morning and then wondering if the coffee maker is off. I'd go back inside to check, lock the door, and wonder if the bathtub faucet is still dripping. They raised the dosage then.

Quarter simply proceeds at a steady pace like a train conductor taking tickets. Maybe she has a line on that different drummer we hear about. It's a shame that she probably isn't collecting data on us, but it's a shame only for us. If she has set her sights low, she is succeeding.

Unless she can't think in those terms. A Russian neurologist once described a woman who was born without all of her frontal lobes. No matter how many times she was served a roll—one immediately after the next—she would cross herself and eat.

The textbook never got around to the ethics of the experiment, though. Did the doctors let her get fat? Did they take care of her once she had served their purposes?

What are the ethics of the experiment that Quarter goes through or the experiment that is conducted on us? The parents or social workers behind it may not hear much of the outcome, but they must know something is up. What do they do with all the change?

There is change. The first timers sometimes chip in, and the aged Black women with Bibles unzipped from well-worn leather cases are good for a contribution to the Quarter Fund about half the time. They are going to the jobs that were available to their generation, and those jobs aren't on the fast track, only an S bus. Today's reading, though, might be the one about the widow's mite.

Students, still shocked that the world is unfair, are the most reliable source. A dreadlocked blond boy straight out of Scarsdale or Santa Monica has no trouble redistributing twenty-five cents, sometimes fifty, of this week's check from home. Just as generous are the girls who wear backpacks studded with buttons that protest acronyms or advertise bands. They shell out because the World Bank won't.

The no inglés vatos of Mount Pleasant, between San Salvador and lunch prep at downtown's kitchens, usually just shrug. Their pay goes to their rent and Western Union transfers, or however they're sending money home these days. All I can pick out from their flurry of words after she passes is something about la china. Triste, they say. Sad.

She smiles and says, "Thank you" when she receives change. Rejected, she just asks the next person like the woman who ate roll after roll.

A lot of these rejections come from white women on their way to work after a few years at a K Street job since their own backpacks of protest. Some, maybe more recently transplanted to DC, are still in shock about the distasteful public aspect of public transportation. Their answers might begin with "Sorry" and end there, but usually there is less cushioning, along the lines of "No" or "You know you're not supposed to do that." Nothing creates expertise in morals and manners like a steady job and a good salary.

Quarter rebounds from each rejection like a balloon bouncing off a wall and asks the question once more, almost sweetly, to the next person in her sight.

Sometimes that person is one of the ruthlessly clean-cut twenty-five-and-unders in suit and tie. Some are congressional staff and proud of it. Others carry bags and wear lapel pins with the Procrustes Institute's logo or whatever that think tank is whose Latin motto means "Markets are the answer. What's the question?"

When she approaches, they labor visibly. In a silent film, the caption might read, "What would Ayn Rand do?" They know and act accordingly, but they are polite about it. Rudeness is inefficient.

They have a point. I have turned down her request once, and there was no point in being abrupt or giving her a lecture that she might not absorb. I just said, "Sorry" as softly as I could while still being heard above cell phones and headphones spilling out their music.

Maybe she was in it to socialize instead of for the money; she just smiled and moved to the next row. The clean-cut young men definitely have a point.

A point. Hmm. That sounds like it should mean something.

It does. Oh, bloody hell. Oh, bloody, motherfucking hell. I need to have talking points ready by noon for a press conference at two, and I gave myself time to do that this morning, but now that time is getting eaten up by a gridlock that looks like something out of a Godzilla movie where everybody is trying to get out of Tokyo. I left my laptop at home, I have nothing to write on but the margins of the *Post* and the back of an ATM slip, and the only pen I have is blue. Blue ink is for grocery lists. Serious work calls for a black pen.

And I don't have one.

This is what psychologists call a high responsibility, low control situation. Like when I was a bag boy in a grocery store, I was sandwiched between the assistant manager who had found his kingdom and the customers who wanted everything double bagged, some in paper and some in plastic, with eggs on top of everything but the bread. Like the commodities trader on the floor. Like the white-collar person that I am who is one blown deadline away from getting replaced by an unpaid intern and begging for another entry-level job or just begging on the streets in general.

My pulse is up but not from the coffee, and the doughnut hardens in my stomach. Adrenaline is taking over. It's a good thing that I'm sitting in the back. If anyone came up from behind and tapped me on the shoulder, I would swing first and ask questions later.

If anyone approached me from the front—well, no one would approach me from the front. Anyone with half a brain can see that I have a paper in front of me, and if they didn't notice the pages of the business section shaking in front of me, they might think that I was reading instead of producing gastric acid and spin.

But my spider-sense is tingling or my peripheral vision is. There is heat, an aura, and maybe scent. Someone has entered my bubble.

"Do you have quarter?"

Goddamnit! The opening words of my candidate's non-answer slip away. For a few seconds, I am silent, still chasing down greased pigs of rhetoric.

My confusion must look like incomprehension. "Do you have quarter?"

The dog in my mind has taken shelter. There is only a spring, and it has been set off.

"No, Goddamnit! I do not have a quarter." I do not check my pockets. "I do not have a single, motherfucking quarter, and if I did, I would sure as hell not give it to you."

Does she understand what I'm saying?

Does it matter?

Relieved of these questions, I don't have to wonder if I should stop. This must be what abusers feel when their blood pressure drops, and their pulse slows as they draw back to strike. It is the difference between anxiety and certainty. A normal voice is no longer low enough.

"I will never have a goddamned, motherfucking quarter for the rest of my life. I will have nickels, dimes, and pennies. I might even have a John F. Kennedy fifty-cent piece or a Susan B. Anthony-lesbian dollar coin, but I will never, *ever* have a United States quarter for you and maybe not for any-motherfucking-body else."

This feels good. Transcendence of bourgeois good and evil. The liberated id. All those concepts by the French guys I read in college but applied somewhere west of the Gulf Stream and far, far east of Eden.

It means something else to Quarter. She stands motionless and creases emerge from her round, flushed face. She draws one quick breath and then another. She hyperventilates until the motion presses tears out of her. She takes a quick step in my direction, and I wonder how strong she is, but with the next step, she pivots left and drops into a seat in front of me, sliding over to the window.

"You hate me," she says. "You hate me." With a thrust of her neck, the left side of her head strikes against the glass and snaps back. "You hate me," she repeats and again bangs her head into the window.

This time, there is a palpable crack. It works its way through the window, and after an almost made-for-TV delay, blood, more maroon than red, seeps and pours from above her left ear.

"You hate me." She slams again as another crack opens a little higher.

Blood splatters like something out of a boxing match, and all I can do is duck. It's a bitch of a stain. I don't have rubber gloves. I have no way of knowing where she has been, what has happened to her, and what microbes live in her body. What if she bites?

Besides the engine's vibration and the scratchy music spilling out from headphones, the bus is silent in a way like it hasn't been since the days after September 11.

"I don't hate you," I whisper. "I don't."

The spell of silence is broken.

"Oh, no," one woman intones.

Another says, "Look what you did to her."

Quarter is locked into the rhythm of her new ritual. Passengers cluster around her, and handkerchiefs flutter out of bags and purses. A strong man steadies her neck and checks her over. A woman dabs the matted side of Quarter's head. No one has rubber gloves.

The bus wheezes to a stop across from Lafayette Square. This time—I am lucky—the back door works. I don't have to push through a knot of people ahead of me and make an uncuffed perp walk past the driver and down the front steps.

I push the back door open and return to my talking points. The bloodstains on my blue notes are already rusting to brown. I'll be able to work around them and finish the assignment. As if I haven't done plenty for one day.

a social message

When the back door of the subway car strained open and clutched shut, it attracted little attention. Police and maintenance men passed between cars all the time. So did high schoolers looking to break another rule and peddlers of various ages threading the aisles. Some sold candy to fund one or another alternative to gangs and drugs. Soft-spoken panhandlers offered only a hopeless stare.

Others, less soft-spoken, made each car in turn an audience for a social message, consisting of unmerited misfortune—housefires prominently—followed by an appeal for monetary assistance.

Taking a breath that threatened to draw all the air out of the car, the man at the back seemed to be one of the others. "Good afternoon-slash-evening. I do sincerely hope you will accept my apologies in advance for taking up a few moments of your valuable time between our workplace and your home, but I promise to be as brief as possible."

Pages of newspapers rattled, and several songs seeped out of earbuds, but no one spoke. Though the man had not raised his voice greatly, its resonance made him impossible to ignore. He was clean-shaven. He did not exude an aura of unbathed flesh; nor was there alcohol on his breath. His shirt and slacks were clean if nearly threadbare. Slung over his shoulder was a well-worn courier bag.

Palms raised but not thrust out, he resumed. "I would like to take this opportunity to provide a short social message."

"Here we go again," a young woman said sotto voce, rolling her eyes. She shifted her purse from the aisle to the window seat. Other seats stirred as passengers shifted their belongings and hunched into smaller versions of themselves. The principle acted upon was implicit. *Do not make eye contact.*

"Please do not worry or be afraid," the man resumed. "I am not begging, panhandling, or taking up any kind of collection. I am not interested in perpetrating a robbery or any other sort of crime. In fact, ladies and gentlemen, for each and every one of you, I bring a gift that I truly hope you will share with those at the end of your journey today and with everyone in your path from this day forward."

"Oh, God," said another young woman.

Some social messengers complemented their accounts of poverty with crisply printed and illustrated versions of end times, future states, distributing fervent and misspelled instructions on salvation.

"I only want to tell you," said the man, "something I hope you know already. You may have forgotten or been distracted in the course of your daily responsibilities, but I would like to remind you of one small thing."

"This is a big speech for a small thing," another passenger murmured to his seatmate.

The man paused as one who had heard that objection before. "This is a small thing, but it is also a big thing. It is so powerful that I have felt morally obliged—even called—to start this simple statement with a lengthy introduction.

"That statement, though, can be reduced to just a few small words. If you truly listen to the world around you and to each other, ladies and gentlemen, you will hear that you are surrounded by love. Great heights and depths and vaults of love. An immense sphere of love that you could not leave even if you tried. That is all that I want to tell you."

"Thank God," said one of the men behind the newspapers.

"I will not tell you who to thank or what to believe, but I want to leave you with a small token."

A second wave of shuffling and shrinking passed through the car.

"Please accept an unmarked dollar bill that bears no additional message of any kind. I wish to circulate it as freely as the love that surrounds us all."

The speaker reached into his courier bag too slowly to be going for a gun, though a few ducked. He produced a rubber-banded stack of the promised bills, not new or crisp but neat. The bills bore no trace of an exploded ink pack.

He made a kind of bow and offered a bill to a woman on his right. "Please accept this small token of the love that surrounds you."

"No, thank you."

He likewise addressed the man in the window seat, who said, "That's all right. Keep it."

The speaker attempted the same on his left and worked his way up the car, hearing no thank you in so many ways. *I don't think so. Not today. Sorry, guy. No.* Some merely shook their heads or lifted a hand.

The resistance increased.

"Don't want it."

"Keep moving."

"Give it to your mother."

Near the center doors, the messenger raised his voice again. "Please, ladies and gentlemen, I invite you to accept this one small token of love. There are no strings attached."

Voices rose in further terms of rejection. There was no agreement on which obscenity came first, but soon after came the first blow, a slap that made him drop the offered bill. No one reached for it.

The speaker peeled another off the top of the stack and repeated his pleas.

He was answered with further blows: fists, feet, umbrellas, briefcases, and a ladle still bearing a price tag. A tennis racket was brought into play, and brass knuckles flashed out of a pocket. Strangely, no firearms appeared.

From the floor, the speaker restated his offer and stretched out his arms to hold up the bills. They fluttered from his grip like failed doves, covering newspapers and food wrappers, sticking to them with blood.

"Did I say anything about wanting a gift?"

"Here's your gift!"

The train moved slowly due to track maintenance. By the next stop, the car was again still.

The man was not identified for days.

the spotted gull

Thomas was back to see his people for the first time in a year. College was over, and his friends had moved away after graduation. Whether he renewed his lease depended on whether he decided to find work, study more, or go back home.

He walked along the lake with Grandfather, near the house he had grown up in. Grandfather could only speak some of his parents' language but never took on an English name. He told Thomas the first words for different kinds of trees and grasses. He pointed with his shotgun at three kinds of ducks, giving their original names, as he left the safety on. He showed one spot that was still good for fishing since the others had overgrown with reeds after the factory opened on the far shore.

This time, Grandfather pointed at the gulls and gave their real name. "My grandparents said gulls were spirits who weren't ready to leave this world."

"What do you think?" Thomas asked.

"What I think doesn't matter." Grandfather tossed an unfiltered butt on the wet sand and pointed with the shotgun again. "The one with the dark spot on its wing is your Uncle Joseph."

Almost a year ago, Joseph had died. He was drunk on beer and slid off a bridge with a weak guardrail. There was no sign of foul play, no stuck gas pedal or cut brake line. Only in the last few months had Thomas learned that such things could happen, and because of television programs, he watched them when he couldn't sleep. Other times, he dreamed of money.

The bird pecked at a closed mussel but came up with nothing. It drove off a smaller gull from a paper boat that still held a few fries and a smudge of ketchup. With enough attention or imagination, the larger gull's shrieks sounded familiar. It was not their tone or their pitch but their rhythm, like Joseph's breath when he came over to watch Thomas in grade school while his parents were out drinking. He had Thomas get on his knees and pumped into his mouth— sometimes twice in one night—with rank smells and tastes. He felt like he was about to choke on flesh and hair.

Joseph later promised money as long as Thomas didn't tell anyone. He never told. And he never received any money. Later came the fear of locker rooms—he gave up on sports— and the sense that any girl he talked to could tell he was soiled. The campus doctor's prescription lightened the stain but did not erase it.

"What happens to the spirit when the gull dies?" Thomas asked.

"No one said," Grandfather said. "Maybe it joins other spirits, or maybe it just dissolves. It doesn't come back here."

While Grandfather napped in the afternoon, Thomas returned to the lakeshore with lunch and the shotgun. He ate a sandwich and drank a beer from the round-the-clock store. He picked apart the second sandwich and tossed the pieces onto the ground.

The gulls came, at least two different kinds. One bore the same dark spot on its wing. It drove the others away until it was alone with the crumbs.

Thomas aimed off-center and squeezed the trigger.

The blast echoed over the lake. All but the spotted gull took flight.

The gull shrieked with a familiar rhythm, flapping a sound wing and struggling to flap its broken wing as it trailed blood.

Thomas sighted for a shot but then lowered the gun. This was too easy.

The bird shrieked and limped, dragging on one side. Thomas couldn't remember if gulls would eat one of their own, but this gull's cries would help it no more than silence.

Thomas opened a second beer and waited for the crows.

the brick in texas

The traveler carries a brick in his soft suitcase. Among socks, pullovers, and glossy magazines, it is the center of gravity, which would sooner break than yield its shape. The traveler bears the brick's weight easily, but it is badly packed and the suitcase grazes his left leg with each step.

The brick's ash-colored silhouette provoked no response at O'Hare Airport when the security guards passed it under the X-ray. It lay outside the universe of hijack weapons, nowhere on the continuum from rattail combs to plastic explosives. The brick passed through their day's work, along with three pints of gin that did their killing slowly outside of the guards' jurisdiction and the dull disposable razor that a suicide might eye longingly in the night. The guards had no time to guess at the items' pasts.

The traveler carries the brick for the weight of its history. It comes from the newly demolished city hall of his hometown near Rock Island. The brick's color changed in the middle of the walls. The *County Chronicles* note only that construction ceased for a three-month period.

Between the layers, lie the events. For a season, bricks had to meet another need. By night, the town's strong men rolled them in wagons and wheelbarrows to the free love colony outside of town. Bricks sailed through every windowpane, their replacements, and the curtained space once the windowpanes weren't replaced. Others clogged the wells or scraped plowshares. Some were aimed at cows and sheep, landing as hard and clean as a slaughterhouse mallet. The free love colonists lost their desire to conceive any more children or assist in the town hall's construction. By the winter of 1840, they were gone.

The traveler's great-great-grandfather led the siege by example. He hauled load after load of bricks, launched them far into the night, and came to be considered a future mayor.

But no one found out how he would have performed. He hung his whiskey jug on a hook and joined the Mormons flowing west, keeping chaste within his polygamy. When his new people were driven out of Nauvoo, he found himself at the other end of bricks' arcs and in trajectories of bullets. He sloughed off his surplus wives and returned to take over the colony's abandoned farm.

The traveler has no more learned this than he has the recipe of the brick—mix of clay, water, and drying time. Nor did he examine its binding fabric of straw or corn husks any more than he examined the fabric of the town's life five generations ago.

Stepping off the plane in Houston, the traveler carries his own intelligence. No one knows or would know to ask about them. He will lay this brick in his new house outside the city as firmly as he has placed his own alien body in the state. Neither will blend in, and there is no telling whether the tempering of the north will hold them in good stead.

The brick, though, is yellow like the rose in the song; the traveler is half-yellow, born from the wife his father retrieved from Korea. Compounded from a different soil, she could never be kneaded into her husband's town.

Nor could the man. He takes the brick, as the Jews take unleavened bread, as a reminder of travel and not of a place. Neither will it provide the cornerstone of a monument to him. After his days, the brick can break loose from the matrix of wants and recollection for all he cares. It can tumble out as he had fallen out of the town and the attributions that fixed his place there. The inaccurate taunts of chink. The rice served to him everywhere but home.

Having served its purpose, the brick can lie plain and illegible as his great-grandfather's tombstone, smoothed by a century's worth of rain. It can come to rest at any angle, a small obstacle, at most, in an armadillo's path.

foolish time

For no reason, I lose a minute, sometimes two, daydreaming of sex or something exotic like the sunset filtered through Easter Island's monoliths. Nothing else registers. I couldn't tell you if a fly or a man has passed in front of me.

Just as pointlessly, I come to myself and remember what I'm doing. Today it's laundry—a platoon of shirts hanging on a rack. I give them a shake to smooth out wrinkles that aren't there, and one shirt slides out from the rest. The cotton torso turns, and a sleeve swings as if moved by the spirit of a fitter self from the days before graduate school and work intervened.

Fabricating a fiction of muscle around my body, as other men fabricate bank accounts to impress their dates, I would run into Curtis, who dispensed wisdom and sometimes towels. In theory, he was the weight room attendant. In practice, he worked out or absconded with his paid time to the court, palming the basketball and slamming it through the net. It cast a shadow in three dimensions against the cinderblock wall and its stenciled No Dunking sign.

He also found time to see what I was doing, usually when I took my eye off the ball or let the bar lower and nearly press me to the bench. Once, he schooled me on the phenomenon.

"Do you know what that is?"

I nodded. I'd been working out.

Curtis knew. "That's foolish time. Do you know what foolish time is?"

At that age, I still thought I was supposed to know everything and, having no idea, I nodded again. Curtis didn't let that stop him.

"Foolish time is time that's gone like it had never been there at all. It's lapsed. It's like being drunk or being with a woman who leaves you. My years banging—and I mean steady banging—with the Vice Lords were foolish time. I don't know where it went."

He must have gone looking. Two weeks later, discreetly as a stolen towel, he left the Y.

After that, the accounts differ. He was caught in crossfire or was aimed at. His name had been signed in at a homeless shelter. He had killed one man in Los Angeles—or two closer to home—and found himself in Stateville, where days are marked without reference to the sunrise or sunset, and the jail cell's weather doesn't change with the seasons.

On days without a rape or a fight, no event intrudes on the body's rhythms: a breath, a lull, and then another breath. The heart's quick squirms, pisses taken, the dawn of a face over the chinning bar, all ways to count down toward the day, and, if it comes, a door obeys a man's touch and opens.

In this counting, if it's his to count, Curtis might find relief studying law, praying under a new faith and name, or addressing a new audience, losing track of the hours as he hands out towels like those I've folded without thinking. As the laundry basket's handles cut into my palms, and the hangers of my flaccid shirts poke, I wish him all the foolish time in the world.

loaf

A love story could begin in a conference room as easily as in any other place, and the principals did not have to be in attendance. Indeed, they might not have been born yet.

In a US conference room, following World War II, a man of European descent proposed extending economies of scale further into the civilian sector, continuing Henry Ford's work.

Dough mixed in industrial quantities at central facilities, with standardization of quality, could be trucked out to spoke locations and finished in ovens that required only unskilled labor following a simple protocol. In short, bread without bakers.

Accepted, the idea was diffused. A town beyond a certain size almost invariably had a finishing plant that sold fresh bread and rolls wholesale to groceries and supermarkets. Overruns and day-old bread were sold at a discount.

In one of the American Midwest facilities, two employees noticed each other. As employee numbers have many syllables that are difficult to remember, we can call them Mark and Linda. From different towns and high schools, they otherwise might never have met.

Across the break room, Mark noticed a new and graceful girl who must have just started in the office. He hadn't seen her on the floor, and she certainly was not dressed for it with her heels and skirt. A closer look revealed that she was not wearing a ring.

Mark wondered how he might approach her and introduce himself. "Hi, I'm Mark. This is the only job I could get, so I'm probably going to be around for a while. Do you want to hang out?"

Linda noticed him anyway. She observed his quietness and how he would clean up after himself as well as others in the break room.

When only one seat was left at her table, Mark and Linda met. Plain words offered in simple sentences served less to convey information than vessels of affinity. A question about her pendant led to a shared interest in going to zoos and places each wanted to see. Their lists overlapped.

That conversation was followed by another the next week and another two weeks after. This momentum sustained itself, leading to a cup of coffee after work one day. Several days later, an unmistakable date on a weekend ended with a mutually sincere but restrained kiss.

To anyone other than Mark and Linda, the subsequent months would have appeared mundane. They made a total of five visits to three different zoos and one aquarium. They went to parties as a couple and often spent nights at each other's homes. They managed to afford an off-season long weekend at the Indiana Dunes—the destination of a lifetime for neither of them but a change of scenery, nevertheless. They made up a planet with its own atmosphere. For them, the turning of a clock's hands and the lifting of a calendar's pages were infused with an invisible glow. They made references, in passing, to getting a dog together. Mark didn't tell Linda, but he started checking on how much money he'd need to save for a ring.

After six months together, though, their planet wobbled on its axis. Linda appeared in the break room less often, and she worked through lunch. At the day's end, she went straight home alone or to a ceramics class on Wednesday night. He did not know she had registered for one.

For a week, they did not see one another except at a distance, and his calls went through to her voice mail. Once, as he was leaving a lengthy message, she picked up and said, "We need to talk. I've been thinking. About us." She did not see how they could have a future together. She wanted children, and what kind of life could they make for them on her salary and his wages. Could they even cover the veterinarian's bills for a sick dog? Mark was in many ways sweet and wonderful but... She did not finish the statement.

Mark drank through the next several nights. In spite of the hangovers, his bread and rolls met the company's standards. He incurred several burns on his hands and arms after accidentally brushing against hot trays. The pain, which provided a distraction for a few minutes, would require further alcohol by the day's end.

He left notes in her office and mail slot until a friend brought up the company's harassment policy. In this economy, he did not expect to find a better job, if any.

In a weak moment, however, he wrote one more note on an index card that read, "I miss you." He left it on the hood of her car, which now had a For Sale sign. He made sure she would notice the card by clipping it to a loaf of sliced rye that could not be sold because of being misshaped. He thought of taking the package back, but with one final attempt, he could live with himself.

Linda took the loaf home. If need be, she could present it with his most recent notes to provide evidence of stalking. She discussed the situation with the attorney she had begun dating.

"Would Mark attempt to poison you?" he asked.

She knew he was not capable but asked if she should call the police or obtain a restraining order. The attorney advised waiting until his actions became frequent or more extreme. What had happened so far would be assigned low priority by the justice system.

"But what do I do with the bread?" Linda asked. "I can't keep anything he's given me, but I don't feel right about wasting food."

This was an interesting question and a distraction from how the bread had come into her possession. The evening's wine guided them to a solution. She could give the bread to a third party who did not know Mark and who would not taste its history.

That was the theory.

The neighbor to whom she gave the bread asked how she received it and developed doubts of her own. Her husband shared a piece with her, and after his own share of wine, he sang a paraphrase of lyrics from his youth. "Tainted loaf. Oh, oh, oh, oh, tainted loaf."

Calling a friend with a small budget, the husband asked how he would approach the loaf at least metaphorically salted with tears.

"It doesn't seem right to let food go to waste," the friend said. "If you don't want it, I'll take it."

The friend shortly thereafter went through half the loaf with various fillings, spreads, and condiments. Yet even he did not think ahead in this regard, and there was only so much he could eat in a short time. In the dry winter air, the slices went stale, but there weren't enough to make croutons or lay up a canister of crumbs.

To avoid waste, he tore the stale slices into strips and tossed them from a park bench to the waiting birds. Several kinds, mostly starlings and pigeons, pecked and squabbled on the ground. They had taken over the landscape.

counsel

Who wouldn't? Not me. No way, pal. In a New York minute. In a heartbeat—less, a diastole. So, by the time that heart beats again, I would have seized the opportunity. If, in the interests of full disclosure, the opportunity ever came my way again, I wouldn't hesitate for an instant.

I did it once or twice, depending on how you classify things. I, of small science and little love, damned nearly no business anywhere and less profit to show for it. I can't be expected to arrive at a taxonomy of moments allegedly at evolution's peak when minds higher on that summit can't determine how many species are destroyed every day or whether a serial killer should be put down like a rabid dog.

What I know is how it felt to have all possibilities before me as my every cell flexed, whipped out, and quivered in its DNA at the brink of taking the first step of a campaign unequaled in scope by D-day.

Those moments felt like some superscripted exponent of at least two digits when every food and drug in my body had balanced at a great height. Not to say that the feeling wasn't deep. It felt like the most sub-superficial catfish saw a worm of untold amplitude dangled on a barbless hook.

I was that fish in all but gills once or twice, and in mastery of that instant, I was about to take in what would transfigure me. That prospect lay available before me. Beholding that thing, I turned away without thinking.

But that won't happen again. I'm a little wiser, I guess. Sadder, maybe. I'm doing okay under the circumstances of course. It would be one hell of a thing if I weren't.

All I can tell you is that if I were in that situation or one even remotely resembling it, I would jump on it and milk it for everything it was worth. I'd take advantage of it in every possible way until there was no advantage left. I've had time to think this through, and there's no question in my mind.

Yeah, buddy. You wouldn't have to tell me twice.

points beyond

night hike

Almost every man likes to think of himself as a cowboy. An accountant, an oceanographer, a burger flipper looks in the mirror and sees some impossible combination of free agent and alpha male who can ride the range and drive the herd from Abilene to Kansas City if he feels like it.

In that regard, I'm no different from anybody else. I might only be different by learning early on that what I think doesn't match the way things are. I've had boots—Justin and Nocona, calf, gator, and rattlesnake—longer than most of my mailing addresses, but since my sixth-grade class trip, I've known I could only go so far down the cowboy path.

The timing alone was a challenge. To go to an underused Boy Scout camp in Lake Geneva would have made sense in the spring when we wouldn't freeze, but we went right before Halloween, and we did freeze. We were supposed to look on the bright side of things, but we were in sixth grade, and the teachers and counselors weren't. From where we stood, the bright side was at the Playboy Club, where we couldn't get in, and the liquor store, where we couldn't buy beer. The drinking age in Wisconsin was eighteen then, lower than twenty-one in Illinois, so it didn't seem as far off in a twelve-year-old's future. That was as bright as it got.

We talked about how our counselor, Phil, could have bought us beer if he'd wanted to, just like he could lead us through the trails that all looked alike or tell the poison ivy from the other plants. They all looked alike too. A casual god in a hooded sweatshirt and Converse low tops, he could do a lot of things.

The only thing he couldn't do was keep us interested. By Wednesday, we had walked all the trails we wanted to and some we didn't. We were tired of eating beans, and gas wasn't even funny anymore. We built fires that went out after the first breeze and paddled our canoes like we didn't care—and we didn't—from the elbow down. We wanted Ho Hos and a television.

Or at least a little horror.

Doug said that there was a dead cow just outside the camp. Because we all kept asking Phil about it, he couldn't single out anyone for stepping out of line. Everyone and no one was responsible. We were willing to give Doug the benefit of the doubt, even though no one could figure out when he'd had the chance to look. Besides, he could do a lot of things like catch bees with a margarine tub and his bare hands.

At Wednesday dinner, without beans, Phil gave us what we wanted or just hoped to tire us out so we would complain less the next day. Lights out would come in an hour, so we could hike off-trail and look for the cow's body.

"Cool," I said.

Alejo said, "Shit, if I want to see a cow's head, I just have to look in the freezer at my dad's restaurant."

"Who said that?" Phil asked.

No one and everyone. We laughed to cover for him.

"If you don't want to go, let me know before you go back to your tent."

We looked away to see if Terry would say anything. He'd come to school in September from England. He had wide blue eyes, and he was pale like one of my mother's porcelain dolls that had broken when we'd moved from Texas the spring before.

Terry made things worse for himself. He turned away when somebody stepped on the worms that came out in the rain. When we watched films in class, he would get sick after a lion opened a wildebeest or a naked tribesman hacked up a giant millipede. Almost every Friday, the janitor had to come around with his sawdust box to soak up the vomit.

Worst of all was his last name: Timm. Even if we'd liked him, he'd have to be Tiny Timm.

We waited. Then the question came from the middle of the group. "Are you staying, Tiny Timm?" We laughed.

He shook his head.

A second voice spoke in a hoarse whisper that we had taken for sarcasm. "It's okay if you stay, Tiny Timm. We know you want to."

Timm took a deep breath and said, "I'm not staying." The last note went high, and he shook. It wouldn't take much more to make him cry, and it was worth a shot.

We took up the hoarse voice and chanted each line from a different corner.

"Tiny Timm."

"Tiny Timm."

"His dick's so small…"

"It won't stay in."

Phil's question came again. "Who said that?"

We laughed and acquitted ourselves again. At this rate, he would never buy us beer.

"Remember," Phil said, "you don't have to go if you don't want to. It's not like I'm going to announce your name."

He wouldn't have to. There were only thirty of us, and if anybody stayed, everybody would know that he had left them at the girl's lodge. Sixth graders didn't get to choose between embarrassment and even an outside chance of danger in the forest. The doctors' and lawyers' kids mentioned a thing or two about liability.

We wandered back to our tents to get our flashlights. The battery in mine was fading, but I didn't get new batteries. I didn't think I'd get to look very long anyway.

Everyone turned out to answer the roll, pushed by the thought of staying in the girls' lodge and pulled by the chance to see a real corpse. Bodies in slasher movies were like cartoons, just with flesh and rubber. Worms didn't count; they didn't even have eyes. The crawfish we poked at in the stream might have counted, but they kept getting away. A whole cow, rotting on the ground, came closer.

Phil led us away from the lake and toward a spur of trail. We walked in small clusters like commandos in a movie. Alejo, Doug, and I walked fast, closer to the front. I was trying to warm up. Terry followed by himself.

Shivering, I crunched the frosted leaves in my path. "I wish it was more like Texas up here."

Alejo laughed out a cloud of breath. "What, you mean like where the Rangers pull your dad over and mess with him?"

"That never happened to my dad."

"It wouldn't happen, Pete." He pointed to his cheek and then mine. We didn't say anything for a few minutes.

The woods ended, and the trail opened into grass and weeds.

"Listen up, guys," Phil said. "The cow is by that clump of bushes over there. Take a look, but don't get too loud or do anything to draw attention to yourselves. This isn't the camp's property."

We followed him. The footing was level, but I left my flashlight on. Most of the others pushed past me, and we made a half circle two or three rows deep. The front row spoke.

"Cool."

"There's still some hair on its head."

"Is that an eye?"

"Why aren't there any maggots?"

He didn't stand there long enough to make sure. Neither did anyone else. My turn was coming soon, and I breathed faster. My temples got sore. Others moved up and drifted back. Doug poked at its nostrils with a stick, and Phil said something about diseases.

Phil looked us over. "Has everybody gotten to see it? Not yet? Terry, take a look then."

The hoarse voices came back. I didn't have enough breath to join in. Someone pushed Terry from behind, but he didn't move.

"Tiny Timm."

"Tiny Timm."

"His dick's so small…"

"It won't stay in."

I tried to join in but only gagged and breathed faster. The pressure in my temples spread to my forehead and my eyes. I couldn't keep track of the chant but remembered the Good Friday service last spring when we followed the script in the bulletin and said, "Crucify him!"

I sniffed, swallowed, and found my place.

"Tiny Timm."

"Tiny Timm…"

Phil broke in. "Come on, Timm. Shut these guys up."

Terry stepped up all at once—the way people tear off a bandage—and simply stood there with his arms at his sides. He didn't point or say anything, but he stood there longer than anyone.

"Okay, Timm. Have you seen enough?"

He nodded.

"Is anybody else left?"

Before I could move or say anything, Doug said, "Yeah, Pete hasn't seen it yet."

I stepped in front of the others and looked. I couldn't turn away too soon, so I came closer and shut my eyes. What I stopped looking at still looked at me. It stared me down even though it was dead like the tadpoles I had scooped up from a marshy field near my school and kept in a jar. They wouldn't eat the fish food I threw in, wouldn't grow their front legs, and wouldn't absorb their tails in time to crawl out and jump away. They just added their flesh to the water's algae stink at ninety degrees in the garage, sinking by twos and fours.

Dead. Like the mussel my father's boss had opened at the company picnic to see if he could. He slipped a knife between the valves, and they opened with a snap. He showed us their small pink cargo, a dot of life, before throwing the shell and meat into the Gulf.

Dead. Like the geckos in our old house. One, dry and clean, hung on to the curtains, stalking an insect that never came. Another, an inch long with black pinhead eyes and see-through skin, fell from the bathroom closet on the second floor. I looked for it and wanted to take it outside, but it was gone, camouflaged against the tile, lost in a crevice without food, or already crushed. By the next day, it would be dead.

Dead. Like, in a box I never opened, the fetal pig my parents' doctor friend had given me when he heard me talk about being interested in science. The pig I could never bring myself to look at, let alone dissect. It was a mammal like us and dead like we would eventually be.

Dead. Like the cow collapsing on an abandoned barn and turning into dirt. I looked again in case anyone was looking at me. One flashlight beam stayed on the cow's head or one side of its face. It seemed like a face anyway, except for the ragged lips that showed where the gums were shrinking back, the softening eye, and the jagged half ear.

The hide was still there, but it didn't rise or fall with each breath. A dark hole on one hind leg stayed dark under the lights, a big period or the mouth of a tunnel. In the rough triangle between the leg and the ribs, I saw another gap that let out bloody mounds of something that had been in the cow and now was left to the air. It was changing into something else.

My insides, that the air or the dirt would turn into something else, squirmed and shook like they were trying to escape. I exhaled as if a giant hand had pushed me. That same hand put me on all fours and made me throw up into the grass and the brush, but I was hit on the back before I could choke. Phil brought me to my feet, and everybody stepped away from me and my breath when I went back into the crowd.

We walked back to camp in different clusters than before, and nobody said anything except for a few whispers I couldn't make out.

We were all finished with nature. On Thursday, we played volleyball on courts scraped out of the grass and brown leaves. Phil made Terry a captain, and he picked me next to last.

I don't remember playing or who won, let alone what the scores were. All that stays with me is how Terry made the first serve underhand and how the ball reached the top of its arc and seemed to stay in place.

In offices, while daydreaming, I still watch for its descent.

big radio voice guy

Designation

In professional circles and along with his given name on flyers and programs for the charity fundraisers he hosts, he is known as Big Radio Voice Guy.

The syllables add up to a burden for mouth, tongue, and ear. Still, abbreviation entails violence, a reduction of possibilities for at least one point in time. In his line of work, the thought of foregoing rhythms and resonances pain him. Yet surgery too is violence. The comparison heartens him, and he explores the available possibilities.

BRVG, whether with or without periods, represents the obvious choice.

Yet it rings false. Four letters assume the heft of a word in itself. Even if four letters don't add up to a word, no one deserves that much of a title. Then again, the problem might be nothing more than the letter *R* with its gear-grinding impersonation of a break in the fleet phonemes. At any rate, the *R* is implicit. He does not have to distinguish himself from Big Stationery Voice Guy or a large-voiced man of ornithology.

The letter *R* falls away, and on his business card, his name is followed by a comma and BVG, as others are followed by DDS or MSW.

Memos and production notes follow suit with instructions, such as "BVG at 10:17 a.m. CST." Clauses of contracts precede those letters with "Hereafter referred to as..." It proved useful in his voice mail as well. Referring to himself as Big Radio Voice Guy had always seemed a bit pompous.

An acronym, though, could be played with like the letters on Scrabble tiles. A message in his current rotation, acknowledging the time or not keeping up with it, states that BVG will BRB. One of his past messages began with the paraphrased musical question—Are you down with BVG?—until the musical reference became dated, which took a surprisingly long time.

The Stations of the Voice

Big Radio Voice Guy can be heard on two hundred stations across North America and more than three hundred if considering HD radio affiliates. Most of those stations' letters start with *W*s, though some begin with *K*s and even a few *C*s. Some identify themselves with spirit animals as well.

Those stations primarily cluster around the US side of the Great Lakes, becoming less dense with population and as local cultures shade into other speech patterns. West of the Rockies, English-speaking natives want to hear low and slow tones like their own voices or something pastel sounding on the coast. In the presence of the Rockies and the Pacific, there is no point in competing with them. The South remains itself.

Ontario at its most expansive and friendly remains unwilling to call undue attention to itself unless the subject turns to hockey, a sport BVG knows only superficially. He has repeatedly tried without success to understand icing and why it is a bad thing. Quebec remains, as it insists, French. A language borne on torrents of vowels and nasals has no place for a non-native speaker who leans hard into his consonants when he isn't grinding them.

Mexico dangles from the lower forty-eight and in his imagination like a broadcasting cluster of grapes. He cannot reach them, but he is sure that they are not sour. Long gone are the days of Wolfman Jack, with fifty-thousand-watt transmission and a five hundred mile listening area on either side of the border. But this is not what troubles him. BVG is fluent in Spanish with only a slight accent. High school and college classes by day and restaurant jobs at night laid the foundation.

But Mexico did not need him. On several occasions, his agent had made inquiries but always received the same answer. Vatos de voz grande represented the norm there, and they worked cheap. BVG need not apply.

If the mountain would not let him climb, he could still scale a year. For a year and over his agent's objections, he provided station identification for a ranchera and norteño frequency in southern Ohio. To his agent's relief, he declined to renew his contract as the playlist shifted toward narcocorridos. The principle meant more to him than the challenge. Shortly thereafter, the station changed hands and became an English-language subsidiary of a ministry named after someone still walking the Earth.

With Laryngitis

Far worse could befall him. There's no need to invoke the remote specter of cancer. BVG has no family history, and he does not smoke. Vocal cords can accrete nodes though, if not tear or snap, but this has yet to happen.

Instead, two or three times a year after dreams of no particular sort, he awakes capable of no more than a croak. After a few words, not even that. At most, he can whisper to those who draw close.

Then all bets are off. All appointments are canceled. More than once, he has sent away an airport limousine driver with a sign in broad marker strokes and a sizable tip to dull the sting of a dry run.

What remains for him to do? He sends emails whose subject line includes the word *regrets*, and he lets calls go to voice mail. Tension ebbs from his furthest extremities and the rest of his body. After two decades, he still knows performance anxiety and stage fright despite the invisibility of the studio because he wants to fulfill his contractual obligations and because he can be replaced by any number of applicants.

With the tension gone, he naps, no matter how much coffee he's had.

For the next two to four days, he only walks his dogs during the day, ingests various soothing liquids in all his waking hours, and plays charades with his wife and children in the evening. Mostly, he listens to classic rock and eighteenth-century classical music on vinyl. He yields the floor to a good half dozen species of birds at the feeder or to squirrels' scolding. In warm weather, he yields to hummingbirds' wings near the back yard's bright flowers.

At no point must he answer. Nothing is demanded of him. A second take can't be done in the absence of a first.

If bliss can be imagined as a country, these spells represent its most scenic province for him.

Signs of Promise

From birth, he was a good (i.e., quiet) baby, who almost slept through the night. As he approached the one-year mark, he babbled and cooed, as is customary, but even more so.

Only when words came did problems arise. Without anger and with impeccable grammar, he would ask, "May I please have a cookie?" or say, "I would like to have a dog!" and be heard all over the house. He had to be made fit for society.

Shortly after his fifth birthday, his mother started asking him to use his inside voice.

He replied, "I DON'T HAVE AN INSIDE VOICE!"

He could not be contained, let alone silenced. He could only be located.

Advice to the Young

BVG hates interviews and always has. There is no script.

A good interview question, one that usually starts with a question word and doesn't simply ask for a yes or no answer, can be answered in any number of ways, all of which takes time and effort. Besides, the answer has to be longer than the question itself.

The wisdom of engineering majors in college comes to mind. The more parts something has, the more ways and places it can go wrong. And interviews don't have second takes.

Now and then, though, other considerations loom larger than his comfort. In spite of turning down several previous requests, he once gave in to the alumni magazine after reading about a third straight year of budget cuts and the elimination of another language degree program. In addition to a larger donation than usual, lending his name couldn't hurt.

The telephone call went smoothly enough until the interviewer, herself a recent alumna, asked what he would tell anyone starting out in his field.

"Let me go off the record for a minute," he said. "You are kidding, right? I'm just an announcer, and the world's a lot different from when I started out. A handful of companies control everything now, and if they don't like your style, the only work you might find is DJing weddings."

He listed them, and she noted that one of them was a major donor to the business school.

"If you give me a few days, I'll try to come up with something you can print."

She agreed, and he emailed his response:

First, don't follow in my footsteps. I still have some good years left, and I can do without the competition.

Second, don't. Seriously. There aren't that many jobs, and they're not as glamorous as they sound. Worse, you might get bored.

Also, don't smoke. Nobody should be doing that anyway. Besides, for better or for worse, raspy voices aren't going to make a comeback any time soon.

Finally, read a lot. Newspapers, history, Russian novels, etc. Whatever you can get your hands on. That will make you thoughtful, and listeners will pick up on that. The guys who don't read always come off as shallow, like there's something missing because there is. And it's always the guys. Women in this line of work read.

From a Conference Call Transcript

We got our ass handed to us in the last Arbitron.

That we did.

So, what are we gonna do about it?

Bum out?

I think we're checking that box right now. Next.

Who the hell says it has to be a popularity contest? It's a business. If we can't raise our ratings, we can cut our overhead.

And how do you want to do either one of those?

First, we can change our format. Maybe do hip-hop.

We don't know dick about hip-hop. Anybody who can program that can ask for more than we can afford.

That brings us to the second part then. Where can we cut expenses?

Vending machines instead of free sodas.

The DJs spring for their own hookers.

Wiseass.

What aren't we doing in house?

The bumps: station identification, DJ identification...

What's that?

You are new to this business, aren't you? You've heard bumps. You know, you are listening to dead-ended broadcast major, Joe Dickhead.

Harsh.

It's true.

I didn't say it wasn't. So, who's doing that for us?

Big Voice Guy.

He's still around?

He's not that old. He's just been doing it forever.

Seems like it, anyway.

How much does he cost us?

Lots. Let me have the intern dig that up... Yeah, Jeff, the coffee's just the way I like it. Now, I need you to check out a number.

Before we get too far, what are the alternatives?

There's that kid who's been doing the West Coast markets.

Too laid back. He always sounds like he's a bong hit from naptime.

How about that guy on Long Island?

Hell no. He sounds like a puppy getting shocked in the nads.

And how do you know?

I'm just guessing here.

Right.

And how much do they go for?

Whatever they want. Their agents are in a pissing match.

Figures.

Jeff just came back with some stuff from the databases. Kid's some kind of Harry Potter with this shit.

So, what's he got?

I'm not sure BVG is any cheaper than the other guys, but he doesn't seem to be holding out for any more than he's getting now.

No pissing match, then?

He apparently prefers to urinate alone.

I take comfort in that. What else should we know?

For the last two years, the focus groups have given him higher positives and lower negatives than anything else. Not the DJs, not the format, and not the commercial scheduling.

If it ain't broke…

Maybe we re-up him for another year and go over to a Jack format. All the people yammering on their cell phones while they drive aren't listening to the DJs anyway.

Let's do this thing one step at a time.

Okay. Everybody who wants to keep BVG for another year, raise their hands.

Um, we're not teleconferencing.

Good point. Let's call the roll.

In Person

As familiar as his voice may be to millions, he is seldom recognized in person. His last head shots were taken at least a decade ago, and no one has asked for new ones. He can dine undisturbed at any restaurant in New York or Los Angeles. On a handful of occasions, he has appeared on a baseball stadium's Jumbotron, but the crowd cam did not linger, and there seemed to be no applause for him.

The last time anyone stopped him by saying, "Aren't you…" was four years ago outside the Royal Ontario Museum in Toronto. And it turned out that he wasn't. The woman had thought he looked like her high school bus driver.

Roads Not Taken, One

The question had dogged him since adolescence. Every speaker began with more or less the same compliment. "You speak in such a wonderful tenor. Have you ever thought of singing?"

This depended on what people meant by singing. Of course, he sang. How many people didn't? The shower afforded him the same acoustical cave as anyone else and singing along with the car radio made the miles go faster between his college and his parents' house.

The people who offered their praise and asked that question suggested that this did not count. They meant singing in front of an audience on a stage, carrying a tune for those who could not do so themselves, and giving color to the words lifted off the page and committed to memory.

The pressure mounted from several sources: a guidance counselor, a great-aunt, and a church choir leader. The director of his high school choir added the last straw. He could audition for the choir or be reported for smoking outside before first period.

For weeks, he pored over the songbooks, trying to memorize the lyrics and make sense of how the dead black notes translated into the tunes he didn't know, let alone the ones he did. His shower singing found a focus. Turning the radio off might have helped, but with an allowance of five dollars a week he couldn't buy many records. How else could he hear the lesser hits of *Saturday Night Fever* or get to know Texas Swing? Every few minutes, he held one tune in his mind, briefly two, and then none.

Several times during this stretch, his mother would say, "It's almost time for dinner. Why are you staying in your room?"

"I'm getting ready to try out for the choir."

"That's nice."

It could have been. After school on the appointed day, he lined up and waited his turn with sheet music in hand. When he was called, he brought up his music and stood without singing or speaking.

"What are you doing?" the choir director asked.

"I'm waiting for your instructions."

"No. No. *No.* I mean what are you doing with that sheet music? You should have it memorized. Set the music down."

He complied.

"Not on the piano. Put it on a chair."

145

He complied again.

"Now, Marlboro Man, you will sing 'Ode to Joy.' I will go easy on you. Sing the English version."

How hard could this be? It was a short song, and there was something about joy in it. People were watching him, and his mind went to a place without words, like the time he had taken a line drive in the groin.

"Well, are you singing or just wasting everybody's time further?"

He sang, "Joy O Joy is where it's at. So, get yourself some Joy. Go cat…" He finished the verse with a handful of stutters and further improvised lines with an impersonation of Dean Martin.

Faint clapping came from a student in the back of the room. Then silence.

"If I had the page in front of me, I could have nailed it."

"That will do, Joe Camel. That will do. I am sorry you did not take this opportunity more seriously. You are free to go."

He left the music room and reached the bathroom before vomiting. He was reported after all. His parents grounded him, and his allowance was halved for a month. He never picked up a cigarette again, and his agent would later mention how clients appreciated how little his voice had aged over the years.

Some twenty-five years later, he found himself feeling vaguely generous after a Thanksgiving dinner of heirloom breed turkey and a rich Zinfandel that he could afford without a second thought. He considered writing the director a letter of thanks for steering him away from tobacco. Over the weekend, he found the director's address, which turned out to be a nursing home. But by next Thursday, the inspiration faded. If he still had his faculties left, he would take the note as one final press of the thumb, and BVG saw no point in giving him that satisfaction. Bastard.

Roads Not Taken, Two

The caller ID said it was his agent, who only called on Wednesday afternoons, but it was seven forty-five a.m. on a Tuesday. His alarm would go off at nine thirty, the way it had for a decade. Then again, her mother had been in poor health for the last several months, and an emergency might have forced her to call at an off time.

He removed his sleep mask and picked up. Her mother's condition had improved as it turned out, and she had no travel plans besides her usual August fortnight to Martha's Vineyard. But for him, there was big news: a morning drive-time slot in New York with an initial salary in the mid-five figures and ratings-based incentives.

"That's just their initial offer," she continued. "If they want you that badly, we can get them to come up on the money and put you up somewhere while you pick out a new place."

He took a vitamin and finished the glass of water on his nightstand while she proposed a game plan and asked if he was on board.

"I have one question."

"Shoot."

"What time would I have to get up?"

"Let's backtrack. The on-air shift starts at six, and you're looking at about an hour of prep work before that, so realistically you're looking at starting your day at three or maybe three thirty if you live close to the studio."

"You're kidding, right?"

"No, babe. This is the real deal."

He reminded her that he hadn't gotten up before nine thirty in the last twenty years for anything but taking his wife to the hospital to have babies. It worked out better for everybody that way. Totaling the Duster on the way to an eight a.m. class before the coffee kicked in had put off early rising for good.

"We can make sure they know you're sacrificing. They'll find a way to make it worthwhile. They can always find a little more."

"They don't have enough money."

"Now you're kidding."

"Seriously, they don't print enough money." Uprooting the kids to a new high school wasn't going to happen, and the kitchen was finally remodeled. He wasn't getting up at three thirty. He could not go for that. "No can do."

A certain reserve crept into her voice for the rest of the call, and it remained there for at least a year, leaving only when she landed the chance of a lifetime for another client. That success apparently covered a multitude of others' sins.

Though the nine thirty a.m. reveille stood, he would, in the way of aging men, rise in the small hours to relieve himself or to have a glass of water. Now and then, as he rose to meet those needs, the clock read three or three thirty a.m.

Why in the world would people choose to get up at that ungodly hour when they didn't have to milk cows or do some other urgent task? *Madness.*

He answered nature's call, and in ten minutes, he was back to sleep.

Occasionally, at Social Functions

Practical jokes had never appealed to him. Even as a child, he could not watch *Candid Camera*, and he asked his parents why the mean man got to be on television. In the fullness of time, he came to understand that not everyone shared his sensitivity, and some welcomed rude surprises.

With this in mind, in the years after the children left the house, he found a way to reduce if not eliminate the boredom lurking in benefits and receptions.

"Come over here," he said, waving to an individual who was selected carefully and sometimes days in advance. "I have something to tell you."

His interlocutor in place, he said, "This is a delicate matter. I'd better whisper or use my inside voice."

Confused but receptive, the listener would wait as he cupped a hand to their ear,

After taking a deep breath, he announced, "NOW, COMING TO YOU LIVE AND DIRECT ON AM, FM, HD RADIO AND ACROSS THE COUNTRY NOTHING BUT THE BIGGEST AND GREATEST HITS... HITS... HITS."

The pranked party jumped or stepped back, furrowing a brow or rolling their eyes but inevitably laughed. "I should have known."

With plenty of air left in lungs, he did not just laugh. He roared.

the last

I don't go out every night. I haven't for decades. To do so would be frivolous, a conspicuous consumption of time. Knowing how much I have, I am past needing to prove that fact to others.

At this point, not only do I not have to go out every night, but I also don't want to go out every night. I can sit quietly in my room all evening and into the next day.

One could say my existence, unique if not distinguished, is an experiment like anyone else's life. The independent variable is each day's data, commonly known as experience. Data points increase arithmetically, while the relationships among those points increase exponentially. Patterns emerge from these connections, and from these patterns, other patterns, in turn, reveal themselves. The accumulation of these patterns is often referred to as wisdom.

It would be mistaken to say that I, myself, am wise as if I could possess a quality that exists independently of myself, assuming, of course, that there even is a meaningful self behind the linguistic conventions of *I*, *you*, and so forth. Wisdom is something one partakes of, drinks as a liquid. This uptake, nonetheless, takes time. I've had worlds of it, but only recently have I come to realize what I understand, however little that is.

Many never have the opportunity. In fact, one philosopher proposed that humanity's most important project was to increase longevity. Otherwise, history would never transcend the procession of youthful mistakes it had been thus far. For a time, infected with an idea, I took this to mean that as many as possible should share my condition. To this day, I cannot bring myself to say *lifestyle*.

This was before I learned that beyond small favors, such as holding a door open, one can never really do anything for anyone else. Capacities are expanded, but how others choose to use those capacities remains mysterious. It seems as if different principles apply to everyone. Anyone lucky enough to live for a certain length of time might learn what those particular principles are and fulfill whatever they allow.

A sponge could live ten thousand years, but it would never grow wings and fly. Its descendants might, but at that point, they will be called something else. Nor will that sponge ever bear avocados, though I suspect a geneticist somewhere is working on the proposition in an attempt, or better said *another* attempt, to make a second draft of nature.

Then again, I have made the same mistake. At times, I brought others to my way of being with the hope of turning them away from gambling or drinking and toward realizing their potential in the arts. The former projects had some success very occasionally, but the latter had none.

I always reached dancers too late. Neural circuits of rhythm and balance are laid down at an early age. Their tendons shortened; the long bones' growth plates closed. Other artists I tried to help produced little or nothing, and from what I saw, nothing was frequently preferable. Every one of them, however, had complained about the brevity of their days at considerable length. Writers were, as in so many other areas, the worst.

We must come to accept these things no less than the sphericity of the Earth. Just as persons with albinism—and I—cannot sunbathe.

With this wisdom, I stay in, saving myself and others a great many problems, accomplish a few small tasks, and contemplate. The verb usually calls for an object but to name one object precludes all others, and I wish, above all, to encompass. I would have worlds—galaxies—fit into my skull, where theories would race untold laps like particles in an accelerator ring.

It still amazes me that sine waves, for example, should assume forms that vary so greatly among themselves while still recurring with perfect regularity. That amazement follows a year of reading texts on electrical engineering. They described a great deal but ultimately explained nothing. I still have no certain idea as to why some sine waves occur rather than others or, for that matter, why there is something—a universe or universes—rather than nothing. Thinking through these uncertainties, though, I have achieved a degree of precision in tracing their contours. That degree increases, and with it, the skill involved in attaining that degree also increases.

As for me, I still lack the words to describe it. I sense, however, that my pleasure differs little, if at all, from that of orgiasts or gourmands.

My pursuit could be described as cerebral rather than corporeal, but that description entails a false disjunction: all pleasure is cerebral. Both the oenophile and the birdwatcher know what they are doing, and they look forward to doing so again. We find ourselves in consciousness as in a room, and our only pleasure—our only prerogative—is to furnish that room to our taste.

I furnish mine with any number of pastimes. Besides reading, I attempt crossword puzzles but never reach the point of completing the one in *The Sunday Times*. Music goes without saying. There have been great mistakes, such as the organ's invention and the spread of its high afflatus, but the record is largely commendable. Brilliance reposed no more in Mozart's composing pen than in Robert Johnson's dirty fingernails during his brief sojourn in Ontario. (Against all odds, this detour in our respective careers coincided.)

A new experience for me is television. Whether the medium does good or harm remains an open question for me, but I have made a separate peace with it. In fact, I am more than passingly fond of cable. There is no other way to guarantee a steady supply of wildlife programs. I find the wildebeest a strangely beautiful thing, and in the great herds of the savanna, their ridged backs resemble a fleet of low sails. Even though the events have been long since concluded, taped, and edited, I find myself irrationally cheering for them against the lions and hyenas.

Another order of beauty subsists in the cuttlefish. It would be enough if this creature of smooth mantle and cartoon eyes only hovered, merely changing speed and rhythm in countless circuits with other invertebrate flesh. Beyond this, it blushes with a thousand undeserved shames or the hot flashes of an endless menopause. I am embarrassed at my praise, which seems to gush like ink from the cuttlefish itself, but I am continually stunned by its unconscious virtuosity. Few sights retain their freshness so well.

Even closer to my heart are documentaries on endangered and extinct species. Flying things seem particularly vulnerable. The California condor and the whooping crane could join the past with its passenger pigeon, no longer an actual thing but a static matter of record.

Bats, maligned or neglected, face the same threat of being perfected only in their absence, like the mammoth or the giant sloth. Whether these creatures ran out of luck, lost their habitat, or were hunted into extinction is ultimately academic. They now wait in a great receiving line of oblivion to greet those birds, along with the dwindling, deformed frogs. None could vote or evolve as quickly as combines, bulldozers, and saws.

More recently, those who wait have come to include my kind. Strangely, I feel their passing less than that of other species. This sentiment, or lack of sentiment, may seem unnatural, and for a time, this absence will cast a shadow of guilt.

It has faded. A sense of loss is mitigated by knowledge. Some simply do not fight their enslavement to cigarettes or heroin. Some, who have faced no addiction or compulsion, walked into one or another buzz saw out of boredom or on a lark, as if the laws of nature did not apply to them. Thus conclude games of chicken and car races with trains at railroad crossings. In this way, those who know epidemiology like the back of their hands, play Russian roulette with their genitals. And lose.

In relation to such individuals, I experience the same emotion, or lack of emotion, as toward my departed colleagues. A few had always fallen by the wayside, straying too far from shelter at dawn or meeting with a stake driven by zealous villagers. Recruitment still managed to replenish our numbers, and renewed caution maintained them for a time.

The late attrition in numbers, though, partook of completely different qualities. Mistakes were made, and those who made them paid with their own demise. These were not the simple miscalculations of placing a wager on the wrong horse or red instead of black at the roulette wheel. The logic was that of a man who spends his life savings on lottery tickets, believing that he holds the winning number.

But the difference is that the lottery player stands a chance. My colleagues never did, but once a bad idea is injected into a setting, the contagion spreads until its host is destroyed.

Like many bad ideas, the one that extirpated the rest of my brethren came from books and films.

This was strange and distressing, as we had already seen how life imitated art among the mafiosi. Every new film, for a time, was reflected by the gangster public: white spats, followed by chalk stripes, and then the long, pointed collars that plunged like fangs, which marked their wearers as criminals against fashion as well as life and property. The mannered speech of George Raft and Marlon Brando still echoes.

The last ideal I held, the final veil to fall off the truth as I know it, was that my kind were somehow immune from turning into others' image of them. The plucking out of this illusion by its deep root hurt more than any other. The demise of the myth of Progress in any but the technological sense hardly disturbed me; I had long since fallen away from it. After

Antietam and Gettysburg, the sinking of the *Titanic* and the sowing of Flanders fields with blood were merely a continuation. Prime ministers and chancellors might have noticed what lay in store if they hadn't busied themselves with slicing up Africa as if for a cheese tray.

The falling away of my colleagues came as one shock after another. The casualties mounted before I could detect a pattern—the waves coincided with films and novels in which the long-standing principles no longer applied to us. In these works, garlic proved weak as water and crosses were no stronger than any other piece of handicraft. A driven stake held no sting. We were portrayed as able to break through a wall with one blow, as if we had ever greatly relied on brute strength. Some of us were even described as diurnal, an option available to none of us.

To assert these propositions denies a certain balance that underlies experience. An ability is offset by a deficiency. Existence oscillates between polarities, or it assumes the shape of chaos. Reality does not come à la carte.

Refusing to accept this simple truth proved the undoing of those who accepted the new accounts, believing their own press instead of the wisdom that had taken painful ages to acquire. A wave of casualties followed every new book and film.

Thus, some attempted to enter homes without an invitation. Others paraded themselves before mirrors as if no one would notice the absence of a reflection. No less did others still spend their nights like rock stars and sometimes among rock stars, as their thinness and pallor gave them entrée into high society and the nightclubs whose patrons are chosen for their looks. They extended their nights until dawn and beyond. The results speak for themselves.

I still do not know whether to be astounded more at those individuals' recklessness or at their discourtesy. Those who witness the consequences never truly recover. One life would end, and others be ruined for no purpose beyond self-indulgence.

Worse yet, these instances represented waste when there was nothing to spare. These preventable casualties occurred in addition to the normal ones resulting from persecution, especially when the masses were inflamed—as they so often are. Recruitment, moreover, suffered as life expectancies increased. Eternity, at least as an extension of the present, lost its savor for those who had lived through fifteen Olympiads or a second Emperor of Japan. More of the same held little appeal for them.

Those who joined us were drawn from those who would, in fact or metaphor, play tennis on rooftops and blame the air for not holding them up when they stumbled off. The same risk-taking prevailed even after they joined.

Increase gave way to maintenance, followed by a rapid decline. I no longer enlist anyone, taking only enough to sustain myself, because no suitable prospects exist. I see only those who would, in the spirit of their age, plunge headlong into the folly of their predecessors. I neither want to lead anyone to that fate nor repeat my disappointments.

When I tire or am overtaken, a way of life will end. The rest held the prospect of years without end before them to read, to take up wisdom, and to let it rise and leaven, compounding like a creditor's interest. They could have risen to their place as the only natural aristocracy in history, to be honored instead of reviled.

This dream has perished along with my comrades. Instead of turning their strengths and their burdens into nobility, they served nothing higher than their whims. The light brigade of lemmings forced off a cliff in a Disney film could not be blamed, since they could not know any better. But my kind had no such excuse. A vulgar truth can only be said in a vulgar way: in the final analysis, they were assholes.

the urgent, the necessary

The wait for our quarterly performance reviews is over. Besides the relief of no longer waiting, there's a certain entertainment value in the distribution ritual, which is aggressively outdated like any number of similar rituals. At the end of the appointed workday, the director, who has gone gray in a handful of years, stops at our workstations in alphabetical order rather than according to seniority, passing out envelopes signed across the left half of the seal and sealed again with wax on the right. The specifications for this procedure must be guarded among files at a higher level of access, or at least successive directors have come to believe they are and do not question them.

While the director's ritual is a public performance, each of us greet the envelope with a private counterpart. Some tuck it into a pocket or lay it in a briefcase. A few crumple their envelopes, violating the folds, or grasp them at one end like a knife handle as they walk out the door. Analyst Perez sets his unopened envelope faceup on the desk and takes out a bottle of something brown and strong to toast the contents as if to propitiate an unknown god. On more than one occasion, others have helped him continue the ceremony after work. Analyst Barton tucks the envelope into her bra.

Because our actions vary no more than the director's, there is apparently no correlation between how the reports are handled and what the handlers expect to read. *Apparently* is all that can be said because we never discuss our reviews. On the way out, this evening or tomorrow morning, we will discuss the weather. We discuss family, sports, love lives or lack thereof, and even money. All of our small talk circles around a larger silence.

My ritual before not discussing my review consists of setting the envelope under a paperweight and waiting for my colleagues to leave. Then I slide it out from under the paperweight with my left hand, the one I could live without if the contents burn or shred it. I let the paperweight, a chunk of crystal, resist and turn over as the envelope comes free at the usual thirty-degree angle.

At this point, when the envelope is cantilevered like a diving board over a future of uncertainty, I tear open a corner and insert my right index finger. A letter opener seems too impersonal for the text that will extend my tenure for another three months or end it forever. Though I might be difficult to replace since my successor will have a steep learning curve, I am by no means indispensable.

Analyst Montrose came to believe that he was, and he was widely acknowledged as the most brilliant of us all. Six years ago, when he merely skimmed his data sheets, he missed a sudden dip in projected supply and did not activate the protocol for issuing a shortage alert. The official explanation is hidden in thickets of polysyllables, but everyone knows the results as the Atlanta Gas Riot. I last heard he was shining shoes near the ruins of the St. Louis Arch.

I raggedly open the flap and let the contents fall onto my desktop. At this time of day, the landing is audible.

I withdraw the review and unfold it in two steady motions. Perhaps something of this magnitude in my life should blossom like a paper flower in water.

It doesn't. Instead, my recent past and near future disclose themselves as marks on a page. This time though, the review is two pages; along with the usual quantitative section and its twenty items, the optional qualitative section continues at a great length. The comments are handwritten in the director's poor script. Yet, like the rest of this ceremony, these comments are hallowed by obsolescence. All that remains for me is to sign the review and indicate my agreement or at least my acquiescence, a final antiquated touch.

Deciding whether to sign seems to call for no less care than any other part of my work, but the habits of analysis do not end with the turn of a clock's hand as the workday closes. In the last few hours, terawatts of energy have flowed through my synapses as I've allocated them. None should be wasted.

That was the goal, the theoretical ideal toward which our training was directed. No shortages, complaints, or surpluses would produce regional disparities in allowed energy use. Where could brownouts settle and blackouts roll with the smallest losses of life and property?

Our performance could never attain perfection, as our instructors were the first to admit, but we were charged every day with reducing the distance between the real and the ideal. It was better known as Zeno's arrow, forever approaching but never reaching its target.

But arrows reach their targets as we never can. The archer aims at what lies before their eyes, and the target can only move so far before they release the string. We have fewer options. As the image of a star conveys only how that star appeared light-years ago, the data at our disposal summarize a state of affairs that has already changed. Firms expand and contract, or they arise and vanish like bubbles.

We could only hope to minimize the damage. Like goalkeepers, we were given equipment, and our pay was based on performance. We've always paid for our gasoline and electricity like everyone else, but it took little from our sizable salaries. In my first years, when cars were still common, I took drives into the country with no destination in mind. I would be lying if I said I didn't enjoy the speed and the freedom. Or the illusion of it. Those were youthful indiscretions. That's what I keep telling myself anyway. Whatever they were, a man has to stop working at cross-purposes with himself at some point in life. I returned to doing a good job instead of having one.

I circled back to the spirit of our charter class of employees at the Energy Distribution Agency. Once the climate warmed, floods competed with droughts, and stable conditions disappeared. Even hired experts would no longer testify that these were only cyclical variations of the Earth and the Sun or that we had the fuel to make and run machines that would rescue us. At that point, things were not as they had been. Science shaped policy.

We were recruited from the best universities, and our pictures appeared in the leading publications. One called us "Stars of an age of limits," and another described us as "Scouts on the Pareto Frontier." We were celebrities, or as close to it as most people could get, and for people who didn't act or sing, we were paid well. In spite of our means, many of us did not marry, as I didn't. This used to seem like a coincidence, a small random cluster, but over time, the pattern continued as our numbers grew and vacancies filled. What started out as a prestigious job turned into a vocation, and some of us even spoke of it as a calling. Something larger than our happiness was at stake.

This sense of vocation forces me to read and reread the evaluation like a sacred text. As with analyzing data, I believe reading the comments should allow shades of meaning to emerge and guide my next quarter's work. Evidence for this belief waxes and wanes, or it slips just beyond the horizon. Whatever I believe, it is certain that much of Arizona and New Mexico and large portions of Texas depend on me. They are all strangers I have made a point of not meeting or corresponding with. Personal acquaintances would cloud my judgment.

Reading the evaluation, I find the quantitative section neither pleases nor surprises me. Shortages and complaints are up. Temporary surpluses are too, though they are resolved quickly enough. Later records usually show that populations have declined as some leave for land to farm or a place closer to work.

But there is no getting around the fact that my overall efficiency ratings are down. No businesses have closed, no hospitals blacked out without warning, and no one left without supplies and turned to leather in the western air.

But I've seen pictures of what happened in Laughlin and read several accounts. Analyst Burton hanged himself before he could be dismissed.

My incident report section is filled with numbered entries, and incidents are never good. The larger events are accompanied by citizen complaints and bad press. Mine include browning out parts of the Phoenix area, which people don't call the Valley of the Sun that much anymore, to keep electricity going to Tucson. I sacrificed retail in favor of homes both times, but next time, my decision could come down to homes versus homes. Or hospital versus hospital. The existing backup generators are aging, and replacements will take time to install. But that is another day's set of calculations.

From the ink thickets of the comments section arise a few phrases I haven't seen since grade school, such as "seems distracted," "a slowing of response time," and "appears to be engaging in non-work activities." The latter complaint goes unspecified.

Signing off on these comments, on the report as a whole, would take only a stroke of a pen. Everyone goes through peaks and valleys of productivity, and in our training, we were told to expect as much. It is only necessary to acknowledge them, consent to a refresher course or two, and commit to improving performance. Then all is forgiven.

Yet this time, I will not seek forgiveness. There is nothing to be forgiven. At this point in my career, it is not a matter of pride. Analysts either outgrow their enfant terrible stage or move into the private sector. All that prevents me from signing is a regard for the facts. This too might amount to a flaw, but it is less self-indulgence than an occupational hazard. We are all deformed by our occupations, and perhaps our greatest choice is how to be deformed. Rightly or wrongly, I have chosen to be deformed by paying attention and by holding fast to what I see.

The facts behind the evaluation apparently do not fit in its boxes. The largest incidents reported occurred on days when I strictly applied the Southwest Distribution Equation. On days with smaller incidents or none, I went to the edge of my discretionary range and sometimes beyond it. Too many factors lie outside the equation, or the available statistics are out of date. Households are growing larger near the main roads and power lines; a glance at yards and sidewalk on a mild day show as much. Gas and electricity have to follow them. There is only so much we can do for the subdivision holdouts.

As if that weren't enough, the tappers have found ways around the pipelines' sensors, and hijackers more often than not outgun the armed guards on tanker trucks. After drugs were legalized, the cartels had to diversify. On any given day, gas and oil supplies are overstated by five to ten percent. One day last summer, the difference reached twenty percent, and the director took the next week off on the advice of his physician, *physician* generally understood to mean press office.

In recent years, my memos have covered my reservations and confessed my furthest detours into discretion. When there is a reply, in about eleven percent of the instances, my proposals are categorized as denied, taken under consideration, or presently unfeasible. A fourth category— adopted—exists exclusively in theory. I once wrote a memo inquiring as to the ultimate purpose of the equation if it might involve something other than the distribution of energy. Eighteen months later, this memo received no reply. Later replies noted that the issues I mentioned fell under the jurisdiction of the Review Committee, whose mandate was to review the regional equations from time to time. Those times lengthened for a time until the committee was defunded.

With all due respect to the facts, I may initial some of the director's comments. I *am* distracted and move slower than I should. I can lose much of a night's sleep by examining the news and other reports for trends or modeling the outcomes of alternative equations.

Consulting my findings during the day is what must be meant by *non-work activity*, a point on which I will not sign off. This will require an explanation, and I will provide one, placed under a request for extra time to discuss my review.

I have no choice but to prepare the materials now, while there is no noise to distract me save for the low buzz of electric current and the blood coursing past my eardrums. Tonight, I will need to rest if I can while knowing that what I don't learn could change lives or end them. Depending on what happens, even more lives and fortunes could be in play, such as my own. The appearance of equitable allocation might be served by firing me, opening an investigation, or some other burned offering to the public.

In any event, I have no children to provide for, and my own needs are few. There may be work for me in St. Louis.

opening

Frank had come to a good stopping point. Tomorrow would be another day for the report on whether Argentina's leading candy maker could maintain its position in value as well as volume sales. So much depended on how the company could attract a new cohort of entry-level eaters with its Saturday morning variety show. That in turn depended on choosing a new host who could shake her best bits enough to keep the padres as well as the niños watching but not so much as to make the madres change the channel.

None of this was much help for finding something to do on a Thursday night in Chicago. Email to the rescue.

"Jefe Efe, RU down 4 a thang?" read the first email that wasn't spam. Chris might not have been anybody's go-to guy when it came to the written word, but two years out of school, he was already selling some stick figure paintings he called an homage to Keith Haring. "There's a big opening 2nite," it continued. "Nothing o'mine, but U mite rec sum namez. Free snaqs/dranx. Lemme know, dawg."

Frank didn't feel particularly canine, but he wasn't ruling anything out.

The next email that wasn't junk came from Pam. She supported her origami and paper cuttings with an arts administration gig in Oak Park, where she was a go-to guy with the written word. Her messages held no emojis, and after three beers, she would diagram sentences on a cocktail napkin. For strangers. Her final sentence read, "I should take this opportunity to note that Anita, whom I believe you have met, will be exhibiting."

After a few drinks of his own, Frank had once called artists *the exhibitionists* at another opening. Once no one else stood nearby, she had gently corrected him but added, "They are often that as well."

A theme was emerging. Cortez, a poet, said he was going since he had already finished his piece for Sunday night's slam. A surprising number of his poems were about revolution or squirrels—sometimes both—but he never embarrassed himself on stage.

Frank had met all four of them—and a few more— through Eileen, but they'd only been dating for a couple of months when she was offered a ceramics apprenticeship outside of Portland. With no time to get serious, they'd parted on good terms, still talking every couple of weeks. Strangely enough, her friends kept him around. He asked about their work and listened to their answers, and he wasn't promoting any work of his own. He only had to sit back and be cool by association with something to talk about besides leveraging brand equity.

Eileen's friends also saved him from embarrassment. Unlike some people from the office, they didn't try to drag him to places he couldn't afford while he still had to pay off his bachelor's degree from Madison. Good or bad, artists knew they were broke and likely to stay that way.

Frank followed the link from Pam's message: the Gang of More show, featuring both juried and non-juried works from Chicago and the rest of the world. It had thirty-three artists in a variety of media with most works for sale.

It was already five forty-five, and he had to break one way or another. There was no way he could take the L to the apartment he shared in Lakeview to eat and change clothes, train back out to the opening, and get home at a decent hour. Besides, after a day's work, the couch was exerting a gravitational pull. It was best fought at a distance.

The best answer to the invitation reminded him of how a dentist had met his request for a generous use of novocaine.

Sure. Why not?

Walking past The Art Institute, Frank wondered whether one of tonight's pieces would end up in the collection there or anywhere. If the lions guarding the steps had an opinion, they kept it to themselves. In this, they were alone. Pedestrians calling or texting turned the next several blocks into a broken-field play until he took a side street and found an allegedly Irish sports pub. They served Guinness, anyway.

The soup, which tasted mostly like stabilizers, was probably the same tomato Florentine advertised for frozen bulk sales in *Restaurant News*. The fries alongside his hamburger were uniformly cut and probably reached the kitchen by way of a Sysco truck.

A second pint dissolved thoughts of work. The screen looking down on him sized up next Sunday's games with replays from last Sunday's. Several angles of slow motion showed tackles made and missed, a wide receiver slipping past his coverage, and a running back's lateral moves and stutter steps analyzed with freeze frames to see if his ACL surgery had taken as well as the front office claimed. The closed captions stammered on the bottom with spelling that some would put on pictures of cats or children's work on their refrigerator door.

Michigan Avenue threaded through a part of the city that hadn't known what to do with itself for a while, where the South Loop faded from developers' vocabularies and Pilsen hadn't grown north. Without much else nearby, Frank had no trouble finding the venue, a wide five-story brick building on the east side that looked like a place where things used to be made. One of the doorbells near the front door was marked with a fresh strip of paper that read "Here!"

Frank pressed and heard through the aging intercom's fuzz, "You...here...for...art?"

So far, Frank wasn't against it.

Velvet rope with dusty folds and weathered stains marked the path to the elevator. A chute carpeted with red construction paper and masking tape marked the stenciled feet of a ballroom dance diagram with arrows. The freight elevator's cage opened in stages like the mandibles of a huge insect. As it swallowed him, he found another tag in the same precisely careless hand as the one outside next to a button on the wall.

Transported to the fourth floor, Frank found the space filling already. Probable artists stayed within a small radius of grouped works, and younger attendees clustered in groups. Some included faces from the smokers outside the School of the Art Institute or Columbia College. Another contingent of the young stayed close to the works and conferred with each other from time to time; one wore a University of Chicago hoodie. The groups overlapped, for obvious reasons, near dance students of no clear affiliation.

A cluster of backs marked a drink table where Chile squared off against Portugal in a round of wine World Cup, and PBR cans mingled with microbrews in a tub of ice. With a plastic cup of something red in hand, Frank covered a paper plate with green grapes and the last slice from a block of cheddar, still attached to a piece of plastic wrap. A label listed the Jewel price as $4.37 a pound.

The room came into focus. A table near the elevator had a cash register. A flat video screen, mute and black, presided over a doorway closed by a black curtain. He spotted a few faces that he knew by name.

Near another drink table stood Jared, who Eileen had introduced him to, and they had hung out with him during the first couple of weeks they dated. Nice guy. Frank didn't know he was back in town. He'd said he needed to give the salt glazes and geometrics a rest, and he had set out for Oaxaca to get back to the basics. As Frank caught up with him, Chris came over, blond dreads spilling from his cap, and Pam showed up several minutes later. After a refill, it was time to see the art up close.

"Is there anybody we're missing?" Jared asked.

"Cortez, I think," Frank said, "but he always runs late."

It wasn't cultural. An ID check at a bar had revealed his first name as James and his last as something Swedish or Norwegian. Still, he might have been detained by inspiration or a refill of his own, which sometimes meant a second bottle. Cortez could be away for some time.

"Should we start checking things out?" Frank asked.

"Vamos, muchachos," Jared said.

"Indeed," Pam added. "Andiamo."

Already a few picture frames wore the red dots that meant they were sold. One was a black-and-white photograph looking south on LaSalle to street T-boned into the Board of Trade. Another red dot graced a still life in oils of a bong and needles with rolling papers, tiny plastic bags, and a spoon bent into an *s*. Another painting, *Joe*, consisted of horizontal stripes shading down from brown to darker brown to greater depths of black.

"This reminds me of something," Frank said. "It's like a cup of coffee, where you can't see anything at the bottom."

"I think you could bring that to it," Chris said. "Whoa."

"Wait. I think I know who did this," Pam said. "That's Anita's work. Her boyfriend's name is Joe, and he has major depression. He drinks a lot of coffee too."

Other sections of the wall had no dots. A chair with a sharpened rebar protruding from the seat and the backrest was topped with a plaque reading, "Asseyez-vous." In one cluster, each frame contained only the words *actual size* in Times New Roman from ten-point font to a foot high. Some artists liked words.

Larger pieces could be made out at a distance: vague shapes, cloth strips, and straw pasted on canvases, black-and-white photographs of the poor, and an orange textile hanging with a lizard pattern. Heaps of green plastic soldiers surrounded a three-dimensional dollar sign. In a corner, a man played a waltz on a baby grand while suspended by a rope from his ankles. It looked like a good time to refill until a male voice broke from several speakers.

"Ladies and gentlemen—and various combinations thereof—it is with great pleasure that we announce tonight's first showing of the world premiere of the video installation, *Audience Response*, which will begin in just five minutes. Please refrain from bringing food and beverages into the viewing room, as you will need your hands to hang on for one wild ride."

"We should check this out," Chris said. "There's some buzz."

"I've heard about this one too," Jared said. "A couple of the guy's lovers shot it on their iPhones."

The next wall would still be there after the showing, and the next drink could wait. The screens on the wall above were now electric blue. By the time Frank and his party went in, only the front row seats remained.

The lights dimmed, and the same male voice announced, "Please prepare yourself to respond to *Audience Response*." Black curtains creaked open by fits and starts in time with flashes of a white-gloved hand on the left side.

The video opened with a shot of a flat television like those in the gallery but mounted on a short pedestal in a cabinet instead of on a wall. The screen stayed black for several seconds before brightening into a field of static. A scene faded in, blurry from reproduction or a low budget. A man and a woman sat next to each other on a sofa in a large living room, looking over bundles of paper. At short intervals came close-ups of the pen the man held, each time tilting a few degrees higher. When the pen stood at sixty degrees, the camera panned back up to the man, who cocked an eyebrow at his costar.

Within seconds, they were nude and in coitus. Their mouths were open intermittently to moan at what must have been high volume but now muted. As the woman straddled the man and moaned again—this time revealing a dull flash of amalgam filling—the camera panned out at an angle to show a nude man in an armless folding chair and a state of arousal. He turned his head and gazed into the camera.

"That's Professor V," said someone in the back of the screening room. "He says you have to give everything to your art."

"He's sure walking the walk."

Laughter broke out.

"He'd have a hard time walking like that."

Shushing came from a couple of seats.

Another viewer murmured, "Dude, I need to write a report on this. Let me concentrate."

Professor V smiled before returning to his viewing. He pleasured himself and continued with increasing vigor. After the lovers on the couch reached one of their climaxes, the frame shook and so did Professor V, who reached his own and went slack. The video cut to a second scene in the same room. Professor V, still nude, cleaned a patch of tile floor with a paper towel and a spray bottle filled with purple liquid.

"He should have used bleach," said one of the earlier voices.

Others answered.

"Shh."

"Dude!"

"So how do you know?"

The screen brightened. Frank stood as the caption faded in: Part Two. It would be rude to block anyone's view, and he might find out what the piece was adding up to. He sat down again.

The same television screen appeared in roughly the same close-up but now turned on more quickly. The scene began sooner with different actors and coupling in progress. The shot shortly included Professor V, in the same chair and state of undress, but this time, he was topped by a straw boater and grinned more toothily. The pair reached their respective crises, followed by Professor V. Keeping the straw boater on, he cleaned the floor again.

Parts Three and beyond came faster. Professor V wore a beret, Cubs and White Sox caps, and a keffiyeh, among other headwear. He blinked, smirked, and frowned. Each time, the lovers began closer to their climax with different numbers and combinations of sex, race, and body type.

As the man and woman from the first sequence combined again, and someone of unknown sex entered their room in a black mask and jumpsuit, Frank felt the dizziness come on. It reminded him of a bad night of rum shots and bed spins his freshman year, but tonight, he hadn't drunk that much, and he'd been eating. A tremor worked its way up from his stomach to the back of his throat, and sweat droplets formed on his forehead. He shut his eyes and gripped the seat of his own armless folding chair.

This was like being on a boat. He needed a horizon line. *Find it and focus.*

Frank kept his grip on the chair and opened his eyes. The horizon line was hidden in a wobbling shot of legs and backs.

Hang on.

Professor V's hand wiped the floor again, and three women of different heights combined in their own tremor and shaking camera. Professor V cleaned up once more, and the cursor lit on DVD. He sneered like Elvis Presley while wearing a Greek fisherman's cap. His screen showed Professor V alone in the same room where he was now, wearing only the fisherman's cap, but this time, the television was off. A fully clothed young man led a roped goat into the room.

Frank took his chances and closed his eyes again, opening them once the overhead lights filtered through his eyelids. The tremor in his stomach and throat turned into a pulse, and the trickles of sweat on his forehead merged.

Looking for a bathroom, he found screens. The ones above the viewing room entrance offered rows of the same scene like a department store display but in the grainy green and black night vision of combat footage or a wildlife documentary.

The same scene appeared on a television and a wide-screen laptop next to the cash register: a room of people watching a screen. He saw some of the art students he'd seen earlier and one of the dancers—light and expressions flickered across their faces—followed by Jared, Chris, and Pam. And himself. The camera stayed on his face as his brow furrowed, his eyes widened, and his jaw set until his palm rose to his face. The face-palm stuttered on the screens several more times like a DJ's record scratch.

He sized up a path to the elevator. There might still be time.

The actual Professor V, wearing a porkpie and clothes, spoke to a small and growing group around the table. "The split-screen version should be ready in a few days. Advance sales should cover the expenses, and the MP3 will be pure profit... Yeah, one of the biennials would rock, but I haven't figured out who to blow."

"Wait," said the woman to his left. "It's that guy." She pointed at Frank and threaded through the crowd like a running back. He was beginning to envy her skill when she held up a camera at him. "Excuse me," she said after the click and the whine of picture taking. "Have you ever thought of doing performance art?"

It would be rude not to acknowledge her. He could at least nod, say, "I haven't. I'm sorry," and excuse himself by pointing to his stomach on the way out. He could still make it.

But when he opened his mouth to speak, he did not make it. A first wave hit the woman's camera, and a second wave struck some of the phones that had followed. Someone spoke above Frank as he came to his hands and knees.

"Ew."

"This really brings it together."

Someone said, "Poor guy," or was it, "More, guy"?

Frank wasn't asking. He didn't have any more, and his forehead cooled and dried. He spotted an opening and ran. An empty elevator met him, and at street level, he saw Cortez weaving his way to the space.

Frank stood on the balls of his feet and looked up and down the street. He felt like running some more. He could go to Wisconsin. He could go to Oaxaca, the couch in Lakeview, or some other place where things didn't stand for other things. Where things had a chance of only being themselves.

About the Author

J.D. Smith has published six collections of poetry, one humor collection and one collection of essays, as well as the children's picture book *The Best Mariachi in the World*. He has received a Fellowship from the National Endowment for the Arts, and his work in several genres has appeared in publications throughout the English-speaking world.

In other areas of his life, Smith has held jobs including office temp, newspaper stringer, adjunct instructor, grocery bagger and market research analyst. He was the model for the cover art of the 34th edition of the *Overstreet Comic Book Price Guide*, and in 2004 he appeared on *Jeopardy!* Educated at American University, the University of Chicago, Carleton University and the University of Houston Creative Writing Program, Smith currently works as an editor in Washington, DC, where he lives with his wife Paula Van Lare and their rescue animals.

Transit is his first book of fiction.

About the Press

Unsolicited Press based out of Portland, Oregon and focuses on the works of the unsung and underrepresented. As a womxn-owned, all-volunteer small publisher that doesn't worry about profits as much as championing exceptional literature, we have the privilege of partnering with authors skirting the fringes of the lit world. We've worked with emerging and award-winning authors such as Shann Ray, Amy Shimshon-Santo, Brook Bhagat, Kris Amos, and John W. Bateman.

Learn more at unsolicitedpress.com. Find us on twitter and instagram.